☆ INTRODUCING ELSA ☆

Do you like my name? I hope you do like it
or Elsa'll get upset. Do you get the joke?
I tell a lot of jokes because I like to make
people laugh. My family certainly need a
bit of cheering up right now because we've
lost our lovely house, and have to live in a
bed and breakfast hotel. That's what the
teachers at school call me – *Bed and
Breakfast*. But what they don't know is
that I'm going to be a big star
one day . . .

HAVE YOU READ THEM ALL?

WHERE TO START
THE DINOSAUR'S PACKED LUNCH
THE MONSTER STORY-TELLER

FOR YOUNGER READERS
BURIED ALIVE!
THE CAT MUMMY
CLIFFHANGER
GLUBBSLYME
LIZZIE ZIPMOUTH
THE MUM-MINDER
SLEEPOVERS
THE WORRY WEBSITE

FIRST CLASS FRIENDS
BAD GIRLS
BEST FRIENDS
RENT A BRIDESMAID
SECRETS
VICKY ANGEL

HISTORICAL ADVENTURES
THE LOTTIE PROJECT
OPAL PLUMSTEAD
QUEENIE

ALL ABOUT JACQUELINE WILSON
JACKY DAYDREAM
MY SECRET DIARY

FAMILY DRAMAS
THE BED AND BREAKFAST STAR
CANDYFLOSS
CLEAN BREAK
COOKIE
FOUR CHILDREN AND IT
THE ILLUSTRATED MUM
KATY
LILY ALONE
LITTLE DARLINGS
LOLA ROSE
THE LONGEST WHALE SONG
MIDNIGHT
THE SUITCASE KID

MOST POPULAR CHARACTERS
HETTY FEATHER
SAPPHIRE BATTERSEA
EMERALD STAR
DIAMOND
LITTLE STARS
THE STORY OF TRACY BEAKER
THE DARE GAME
STARRING TRACY BEAKER

STORIES ABOUT SISTERS
THE BUTTERFLY CLUB
THE DIAMOND GIRLS
DOUBLE ACT
THE WORST THING ABOUT MY SISTER

FOR OLDER READERS
DUSTBIN BABY
GIRLS IN LOVE
GIRLS IN TEARS
GIRLS OUT LATE
GIRLS UNDER PRESSURE
KISS
LOVE LESSONS
MY SISTER JODIE

ALSO AVAILABLE
PAWS AND WHISKERS
THE JACQUELINE WILSON
CHRISTMAS CRACKER
THE JACQUELINE WILSON
TREASURY

✭ ABOUT THE AUTHOR ✭

Jacqueline Wilson is one of Britain's bestselling authors, with more than 38 million books sold in the UK alone. She has been honoured with many prizes for her work, including the Guardian Children's Fiction Award and the Children's Book of the Year. Jacqueline is a former Children's Laureate, a professor of children's literature, and in 2008 she was appointed a Dame for services to children's literature.

Visit Jacqueline's fantastic website at
www.jacquelinewilson.co.uk

Jacqueline Wilson

ILLUSTRATED BY NICK SHARRATT

The Bed and Breakfast Star

CORGI
YEARLING

CORGI YEARLING

UK | USA | Canada | Ireland | Australia
India | New Zealand | South Africa

Corgi Yearling is part of the Penguin Random House group of companies
whose addresses can be found at global.penguinrandomhouse.com.

www.penguin.co.uk
www.puffin.co.uk
www.ladybird.co.uk

First published 1994
First Corgi Yearling edition published 1995
This Corgi Yearling edition published 2016

19

Text copyright © Jacqueline Wilson, 1994
Illustrations copyright © Nick Sharratt, 1994

The moral right of the author and illustrator has been asserted

Set in New Century Schoolbook MT
Printed and bound in Great Britain by
Clays Ltd, Elcograf S.p.A

A CIP catalogue record for this book is available from the British Library

ISBN: 978–0–440–86760–9

All correspondence to:
Corgi Yearling
Penguin Random House Children's
80 Strand, London WC2R 0RL

For Frances Stokes
(Froggy to her friends)

Do you know what everyone calls me now? *Bed and Breakfast*. That's what all the kids yell after me in the playground. Even the teachers do it. Well, they don't say it to my face. But I've heard them. 'Oh yes, that Elsa. She's one of the bed-and-breakfast children.' Honestly. It sounds like I've got a duvet for a dress, cornflake curls, two fried-egg eyes and a streaky-bacon smile.

I don't look a bit like that. Well, I hope I don't! I'm Elsa.

Do you like my name? I hope you do like it or Elsa'll get upset. Do you get the joke? I made it up myself. I'm always cracking jokes. People don't often laugh though.

I bet you don't know anyone else called Elsa. There was just this lion called Elsa, ages ago. There was a book written about her, and they made a film. They sometimes show it on the television so maybe you've seen it. My mum called me after Elsa the lion. I was a very tiny baby, smaller than all the others in the hospital, but I was born with lots of hair. Really. Most babies are almost bald but I had this long tufty hair and Mum used to brush it so that it stood out all round my head like a lion's mane. I didn't just look like a lion. I sounded like one too. I might have had very tiny little lungs but I had the loudest voice. I bawled day and night and wore all the nurses out, let alone my mum. She says she should have left me yelling in my hospital cot and slipped off out of it without me. She was joking. Mum's jokes aren't always funny though – not like mine.

That was my very first BED.

It's not very comfy-looking, is it? No wonder I bawled.

Here's my second BED.

I used to pretend I was a real lion in a cage. I didn't half roar.

We've still got my old duck cot. We've lost lots of our other things but we've always carted that around with us. I used to turn it into a play-house

or a car

and once it was even my castle.

But then my sister Pippa was born and I lost a house and a car and a castle and she gained a bed. I gave it a good spring-clean for her and tried to make it as pretty as possible, but I don't think she really appreciated it.

Pippa did a lot more sleeping and a lot less yelling than me. She's not a baby now. She's nearly five. Half my age. She's not half my size though. She's not a little titch like me. She'll catch me up soon if I don't watch out.

I've also got a brother, Hank. Hank the Hunk. He had the duck cot too.

He only fitted it for five minutes. I'm tiny and Pippa is tall but Hank is enormous. He's not just long, he's very wide too. He's still not much more than a baby but if you pick him up you practically need a crane and if you put him on your lap you get severely squashed. If you stand in his way when he comes crawling by, then you're likely to get steam-rollered.

Pippa and Hank aren't my proper sister and brother. They're halves. That sounds silly, doesn't it. As if they should look like this.

We've all got the same mum. Our mum. But I've got a different dad.

My dad never really lived with Mum and me. He did come and see me sometimes, when I was little. He took me to the zoo to see the real lions. I can remember it vividly though Mum says I was only about two then. I liked seeing those lions. My dad held me up to see them. They roared at me, and I roared back. I think I maybe went on roaring a bit too long and loud. My dad didn't come back after that.

Mum said we didn't care. We were better off without him. Just Mum and me. That was fine. But then Mum met Mack. Mack the Smack. That's not a joke. He really does smack. Especially me.

You're not supposed to smack children. In lots of countries smacking is against the law and if you hit a child you get sent to prison. I wish I lived in one of those countries. Mack smacks a lot. He doesn't smack Pippa properly, he just gives her little taps. And he doesn't smack Hank because even Mack doesn't hit babies. But he doesn't half whack me. Well, he doesn't *always* smack. But he lifts his hand as if he's going to. Or he hisses out of the side of his mouth: 'Are you asking for a good smacking, Elsa?'

What sort of question is that, eh? As if I'd prance up to him and say, 'Hey, Uncle Mack, can I have a socking great smack, please?'

Mum sometimes sticks up for me. But sometimes she says I'm asking for it too. She says I give Mack a lot of cheek. I don't. I just try out a few jokes on him, that's all. And he doesn't ever get them. Because he's thick. Thick thick thick as a brick.

I don't know why my mum had to marry him. And guess who got to be the bridesmaid at their wedding! Mum wanted me to wear a proper long frilly bridesmaid's frock but it looked ever so silly on me. My hair still sticks out all over the place like a lion's mane and my legs are so skinny my socks always wrinkle and somehow they always get dirty marks all over them and my shoes go all scuffed at the

toes right from when they're new. The brides-
maids' frocks in the shop were all pale pink
and pale blue and pale peach and pale lilac.
Mum sighed and said I'd get my frock filthy
before she'd had time to get up and down the
aisle.

So we forgot about the frock and Mum
dressed me up in this little black velvet jacket
and tartan kilt because Mack is Scottish. I even
had a sprig of lucky Scottish heather pinned to
my jacket. I felt like I needed a bit of luck.

Mack moved in with Mum and me after the
wedding. After I grew out of the duck cot I used
to share the big bed with Mum and that was
fun because there was always someone to chat
to and cuddle.

That was my third BED.

But then Mack got to share the big bed with Mum and I had a little campbed in the living-room. BED number four. And I kept falling out of it every time I turned over at first. But I didn't mind that campbed. I played camping.

But it was really too cramped to play camp. We only had a little flat and Mack took up so much *space*.

There certainly wasn't going to be room for a new baby too. (That was Pippa. She wasn't born then. She was just a pipsqueak in Mum's tummy.) Mum had our name down for a bigger council flat but the waiting list was so long it looked like we'd be waiting for ever.

Then one of Mack's mates up in Scotland offered him a new job up there so he went back up to Scotland and we had to go too. We stayed with Mack's mum. I was scared. I thought she might be like Mack.

But she wasn't big, she was little. She didn't smack, but she wasn't half strict all the same. I wasn't allowed to do anything in her house. I couldn't even play properly. She wouldn't let me get all my toys out at once. She said I had to play with them one at a time.

So I started playing with some of her stuff. She had some lovely things – ornaments and photo albums and musical boxes. I didn't break anything at all but she still went spare.

'You're no allowed to go raking through my things! Away and watch the television like a good wee bairn.'

That's all you were supposed to do in her house. Watch the telly. We watched it all the time.

My Scottish sort-of Gran wasn't so bad though. She did pass the sweets round while we were watching her telly. She called them sweeties.

'Are you wanting a sweetie, hen?' she'd say to me.

And I'd go cluck-cluck-cluck and flap my arms and she'd laugh and say I could be awful comic when I wanted. On Sundays we had special sweeties, a home-made fudge she called tablet. Oh, that tablet. Yum yum YUM.

I could eat tablet all day long. I didn't eat much else at my sort-of Gran's. She said I was a poor wee bairn who needed fattening up but she kept giving me plates of mince and tatties. I don't like mince because it looks as if someone has already chewed it, and I don't like mashed potatoes because I'm always scared there's going to be a lump. So I didn't eat much and she got cross with me and Mum got cross with me and Mack got cross with me.

The worst bit about living there was the bed. BED number five. Only it wasn't my bed, it was my sort-of Gran's. I had to share it with her. There wasn't room in her bedroom for my campbed, you see, and she said she wasn't having it cluttering up her lounge. She liked it when I stopped cluttering up the place too. She was always wanting to whisk me away to bed early. I was generally still awake when she came in. I used to peep when she took her corset off.

She wasn't so little when those corsets were off. She took up a lot of the bed once she was in it. Sometimes I'd end up clutching the edge, hanging on for dear life. And another thing. She snored.

We were meant to be looking for our own place in Scotland but we never found one. Then my sister Pippa got born and Mack fell out with his pal and lost his job. Mum got ever so worried. She didn't get on very well with my sort-of Gran and it got worse after Pippa was born.

So we moved back down South and said we were homeless. Mum got even more worried. She thought we'd be put in a bed-and-breakfast hotel. She said she'd never live it down. (Little did she know. You don't have to live it down. You can live it *up*.)

But we didn't get put in a bed-and-breakfast hotel then. We were offered this flat on a big estate. It was a bit grotty but Mack said he'd fix it up so it would look like a palace. So we moved in. It was a pretty weirdo palace, if you ask me. There was green mould on the walls and creepy-crawlies in the kitchen. Mack tried slapping a bit of paint about but it didn't make much difference. Mum got ever so depressed and Mack got cross. Pippa kept getting coughs and colds and snuffling, because of the damp.

I was OK though. My campbed collapsed once and for all, so I got to have a new bed.

BED number six. It had springs and it made the most wonderful trampoline.

I had a lot of fun in those flats.
I didn't want to leave.

But Mack got this new
job and started to make a
lot of money and he said
he'd buy Mum her
own proper house and
Mum was over
the moon.

Yippee!

I thought it was great once we'd moved into the new house. I liked that house ever so much. It wasn't damp, it was warm and cosy and when Pippa and I got up we could run about in our pyjamas without getting a bit cold. Pippa stopped being a boring old baby and started to play properly. She shared my new bed now but I didn't really mind that much because she liked my stories and she actually laughed at my jokes. We kept getting

the giggles late at night when we were supposed to be asleep, but Mum didn't often get cross and Mack didn't even smack any more. Hank the Hunk got born and he was happy too.

But we didn't live happily ever after.

Mack's job finished. He got another for a bit but it didn't pay nearly so well. And then he lost that one. And he couldn't get another. Mum worked in a supermarket while Mack looked after Pippa and Hank. (*I* can look after myself.)

But Mum's money wouldn't pay all the bills. It wouldn't pay for the lovely new house. So some people came and took nearly all our things away. We had to leave our new house. I cried. So did Pippa and Hank. Mum cried too. Mack didn't cry, but he looked as if he might.

We thought we'd have to go back to the mouldy flat. But they'd put another family in there. There wasn't any room for us.

So guess where we ended up. In a bed-and-breakfast hotel.

We went to stay at the Royal Hotel. The Royal sounds very grand, doesn't it? And when we were down one end of the street and got our first glimpse of the Royal right at the other end, I thought it looked very grand too. I started to get excited. I'd never stayed in a great big posh hotel before. Maybe we'd all have our own rooms with satellite telly and people would make our beds and serve us our breakfasts from silver trays. As if we were Royalty staying in the Royal.

But the Royal started to look a bit shabby the nearer we got. We saw it needed painting. We saw one of the windows was broken and patched with cardboard. We saw the big gilt lettering had gone all wobbly and some of it was missing. We were going to be staying in the oyal H t l.

'O Yal Htl,' I said. It sounded funny. 'O Yal Htl,' I repeated. I thought of a song we sang at school about an old man river who just went rolling along. 'O Yal Htl,' I sang to the same tune.

'Will you just shut it, Elsa?' said Mack the Smack.

'I can't shut, I'm not a door,' I said. 'Hey, when is a door not a door? When it's ajar!'

No-one laughed. Mum looked as if she was about to cry. She was staring up at the Royal, shaking her head.

'No,' she said. 'No, no, no.' She started off quietly enough, but her voice got louder and louder. *'No, no, no!'*

'Come on, it's maybe not that bad,' said Mack, putting his arm round her.

Mum was carrying Hank. He got a bit squashed and started squawking. Pippa's mouth went wobbly and she tried to clutch at Mum too.

'I don't like this place, Mum,' she said. 'We don't have to go and live here, do we?'

'No, we don't, kids. We're not living in a dump like this,' said Mum. She kicked the litter in the driveway. An old Chinese take-away leaked orange liquid all over her suede shoes.

'For heaven's sake,' Mum wept. 'Look at all this muck. There'll be rats. And if it's like this outside, what's it going to be like inside? Cockroaches. Fleas. I'm not taking my kids into a lousy dump like this.'

'So where *are* you going to take them?' said Mack. 'Come on, answer me. Where?'

Hank cried harder. Pippa sniffed and stuck her thumb in her mouth. I fiddled with my hair. Mum pressed her lips tight together, as if she was rubbing in her lipstick. Only she wasn't wearing any make-up at all. Her face was as white as ice-cream. When I tried to take her hand, her fingers were as cold as ice too.

She shook her head. She didn't know how to answer Mack. She didn't have any other place to take us.

'I'm sorry,' said Mack. 'I've failed you, haven't I?' He suddenly didn't seem so big any more. It was as if he was shrinking inside his clothes.

'Oh don't be daft,' said Mum wearily. She joggled Hank and wiped Pippa's nose and tried to pat my hair into place. We all wriggled and protested. 'It's not your fault, Mack.'

'Well, whose fault is it then?' Mack mumbled. 'I've let you down. I can't get work, I can't even provide a proper home for you and the kids.'

'It's not your fault. It's not anybody's fault.

It's just . . . circumstances,' said Mum.

I saw a horrible snooty old gent, Sir Come-Stances, pointing his fat finger in our direction, while all his servants snatched our house and our furniture and our television and our toys. I was so busy thinking about him that I hardly noticed Mum marching off into the entrance of the Royal, Hank on one hip, Pippa hanging on her arm. Mack shuffled after her, carrying all our stuff. He turned round when he got to the revolving door.

'Elsa!' he called irritably. 'Don't just stand there looking gormless. Come on!'

'What's a gorm, Mack? And how come I've lost mine?'

'*Elsa!* Are you asking for a good smacking?'

I decided it was time to scuttle after him. I squashed into the doorway and pushed hard. It bumped against Mack's leg and he yelled and stumbled out the other side, cursing. I stayed revolving round the door by myself. I felt as if I wanted to go on spinning and spinning. Maybe if I twirled really fast like a top then there would be this humming sound and everything would blur and I'd shoot out into somewhere else entirely, a warm bright world where everyone liked me and laughed at my jokes.

I stepped into the grubby foyer of the Royal Hotel instead. There was a dark carpet on the floor, red with lots of stains. The thick wallpaper was red too, with a crusty pattern like dried blood. The ceiling was studded with pale polystyrene tiles but several were missing. I wondered if anyone went away wearing one as a hat without noticing.

There was a big counter with a bell. We could see through a glass door behind the counter into an office. A woman was sitting in there, scoffing sweets out of a paper-bag and reading a big fat book. She didn't seem to notice us, even though Hank was crying and Mack was creating a commotion hauling all our cases and plastic bags around the revolving doors and into the hallway.

Mum touched the bell on the counter. It gave a brisk trill. The woman popped another peardrop in her mouth and turned a page of her Jackie Collins. Mum cleared her throat loudly and pinged on the bell. I had a go too. And Pippa. The woman turned her back on us with one swivel of her chair.

'Oi! You in there!' Mack bellowed, thumping his big fist on the counter.

The woman put down her book with a sigh, marking her place with a sweet wrapper. She stretched out her arm and opened the glass door a fraction.

'There's no need to take that tone. Manners don't cost a penny,' she said in a pained voice.

'Well, we did ring the bell,' said Mum. 'You must have heard it.'

'Yes, but it's nothing to do with me. I'm only switchboard. That bell's for management.'

'But there doesn't seem to *be* any management,' said Mum. 'This is ridiculous.'

'If you want to make a complaint you must put it in writing and give it to the Manager.'

'Where is this Manager then?' asked Mack.

'I've no idea. I told you, it's nothing to do with me. I'm only switchboard.' She closed her glass door and stuck her nose back in her book.

'I don't believe this,' said Mum. 'It's a total nightmare.'

I shut my eyes tight, hoping like mad that it really was a nightmare. I badly wanted to be back in bouncy bed number six in the lovely new house. I put my hands over my ears to blot out Hank's bawling and tried hard to dream myself back into that bed. I felt I was very nearly there ... but then Mack's big hand

29

shook my shoulder.

'What are you playing at, Elsa? Stop screwing up your face like that, you look like you're having a fit or something,' said Mack.

I glared and shook my shoulder free. I shuffled away from him, scuffing my trainers on the worn carpet. I saw a door at the end of the hallway. It had a nameplate.

I pushed the door open and peeped round. There was a little man in a brown suit sitting at a desk. A big lady in a fluffy pink jumper was sitting at the desk too. She was perched on the man's lap and they were *kissing*. When they saw me the lady leapt up, going pink in the face to match her jumper. The little man seemed to be catching his breath. No wonder. The lady was *very* big, especially in certain places.

'Excuse me,' I said politely. After all, I'd just been told that manners don't cost a penny.

'Come on now, out of here,' said the big lady, shooing at me as if I was a stray cat. 'And don't hang around the reception area either. I'm sick and tired of you kids turning this hotel into a play-park. You go up to your room, do you hear me?'

'That's right. Go to your room, little girly,' said the man in the brown suit, trying to brush all the bitty pink hairs away.

'But I haven't *got* a room,' I said. 'We've only just come here and we don't know where to go.'

'Well, why didn't you *say?*' said the fluffy pink lady, and she flounced out of the room, beckoning me with one of her long pink fingernails.

Hank was still howling out in the hall. Pippa was whispering and Mum was muttering and Mack was pacing the carpet like a caged animal, looking as if he was ready to bite someone.

'*So* sorry to have kept you waiting,' said the big lady, and she nipped round the corner of the counter and smiled a big pink lipsticky smile. 'On behalf of the management, I'd like to welcome you to the Royal Hotel. I hope your stay with us will be a pleasant one.'

'Well, we're hardly here on holiday,' said Mum, wrestling with Hank. She sat him down on the counter to give her arms a rest. Hank perked up a little. He spotted what looked like a very very big pink bunny rabbit and started crawling rapidly towards it, drooling joyfully.

'Please try to keep your children under control!' said the big lady, swatting nervously at the advancing baby. 'I'll have to process all your particulars.'

This took for ever. Hank howled mournfully, deprived of his cuddle with the giant pink bunny. Mum sighed. Mack tutted and strutted, working himself up into a temper. Pippa started hopping about and holding herself. There was going to be a puddle on the carpet if we didn't watch out.

'Mum, Pippa's needing the toilet,' I hissed.

'Shut *up*, Elsa,' said Pippa, squirming.

Mum cast an experienced eye at Pippa.

'You'd better take her, Elsa,' she said.

The big lady paused whilst sorting through our particulars and pointed the way down the hall and round the corner. I took Pippa's arm and hurried her along. We passed the Manager's office. His door was ajar. Like my joke.

We had a quick peek at him. He was still sitting at his desk. He'd kicked his shoes off and put his feet up. One of his socks had a hole.

His toe stuck through and looked so silly that Pippa and I got the giggles. The Manager heard and looked cross and we scooted quickly down the corridor. We had to dash, anyway, because it was getting a bit dodgy for Pippa to be laughing in her current circumstances.

Things got dodgier still because we seemed to take a wrong turning and blundered around unable to find the toilets. We came across a gang of boys as we rounded a corner. They were busy writing something on the wall with black felt-tip pen.

'Don't ask them, they'll laugh at us,' said Pippa urgently.

They laughed at us anyway, making rude comments about us as we rushed past. You know the sort of things boys shout out.

'They are *rude*,' said Pippa.

They were ruder than Pippa realized. She can't read yet. *I* read what they were writing on the wall.

We hurried on, turned another corner, and suddenly I saw one of those funny little lady outlines stuck up on the door.

I don't know why they design the lady in that weird sticky-out frock. And she hasn't got any arms, poor thing, so she'd have a job using the loo herself, especially when it came to pulling the chain.

I was still busy contemplating this little lady while Pippa charged inside. I heard the door bang shut.

'Did you make it in time, Pippa?' I called.

'Shut *up*,' Pippa called back.

It sounded as if her teeth were gritted. I stepped inside to find out why. There was someone else in the Ladies. A girl about my own age was sitting on the windowsill with her feet propped on the edge of the washbasin. She was reading a book. Well, she had her eyes on the page, but you could tell we were disturbing her a bit.

'Hello,' I said.

She nodded at me, looking a bit nervous.

'I'm Elsa. And that's my sister Pippa sitting in the toilet.'

'Don't keep *telling* everyone!' Pippa shouted from inside.

'Sisters!' I said, raising my eyebrows.

'Brothers are worse,' said the girl. 'I've got three.'

'I've got one too. He's only a baby but he's still awful. I have to look after him sometimes.'

'I have to look after my brothers all of the time. Only I get fed up because they keep pestering me. So sometimes I slip in here for a bit of peace.'

'Good idea. So what's your name, then?'

'Naomi.'

'Hi, Naomi. I'm Elsa.'

'Yes, you said.'

'How long have you been here then?'

'Sitting in the basin?'

'No! In this place. The hotel.'

'About six months.'

'You haven't! Gosh.'

I was too busy thinking to carry on chatting. I'd thought we'd stay in the hotel a week or two at the most. As if we really were on holiday. I hadn't realized we might be stuck here for months and months.

Pippa pulled the chain and came out of the toilet. Naomi swung her skinny legs out of the way so that Pippa could wash her hands. There weren't any towels so I let Pippa wipe her hands on my T-shirt. Naomi settled her feet back again.

I looked at her. I looked at the tap.

'I could give your feet a little paddle,' I said.

'Don't,' said Naomi.

I thought about it.

'No, OK.'

I smiled at her. She smiled back. Things were looking up. I'd only just got here and yet I'd already made a friend.

I took Pippa's damp hand and we set off back down the corridor.

'I like that girl,' said Pippa.

'That's my friend. Naomi.'

'She can be my friend too. I like her hair. All the little plaits. Will you do my hair like that, Elsa?'

'It looks a bit too fiddly. Come on, quick.' We were going past the boys again. They said some more rude things. Really awful things.

'You think you're so clever, but you can't even spell,' I said, snatching the felt-tip. I crossed out the worst word and wrote it correctly.

That showed them. Pippa and I skipped on down the corridor and eventually found our way back to the foyer.

'There you are! I was beginning to think you'd got lost,' said Mum.

The big lady was handing over a key to Mack.

'One room for all five of us?' said Mack.

'It's a family room, with full facilities.'

Mack stared at the number tag.

'Room six-oh-eight?'

'That's right.'

'That doesn't mean we're up on the sixth floor, does it?'

'You got it.'

'But we've got little kids. You can't shove us right up at the top, it's stupid.'

'It's the only room available at the moment. Sorry,' said the big lady, fluffing up her jumper.

'There is a lift?' said Mum.

'Oh yes, there's a lift,' said the big lady. 'Only the kids have been messing around and it's not working at the moment. We're getting it fixed tomorrow. Meanwhile, the stairs are over there.'

It took us a long while and several journeys to get us and all our stuff up those stairs.

But at long last we were all crowded into room 608. Our new home.

Tea at McDonald's

I thought a family room would have room for a family. Something like this:

41

Only room 608 wasn't quite how I'd imagined. It was a bit cramped to say the least. And by the time we'd squeezed inside with all our stuff, we couldn't even breathe without bumping into each other.

'Home sweet home,' said Mum, and she burst into tears.

'Don't start on the waterworks,' said Mack. 'Come on, hen, it's not as bad as all that.'

'It's worse,' said Mum, trying to swallow her sobs. It sounded as if she was clucking. Like a hen. Mack calls her that when he's trying to be

42

nice. And he sometimes calls Pippa 'Ma Wee Chook', which is probably Scottish for chick. Hank is too big and barging about to be a chick. He's more like a turkey. I don't get called anything. I am not part of Mack's personal farmyard.

I stepped over all our stuff and climbed across a bed or two and made it to the window. It was probably a good thing it had bars, especially with Hank starting to pull himself up. He'd be able to climb soon and he's got so little sense he'd make for the window first thing. But I didn't like the bars all the same. It felt as if we were all in a cage.

It wasn't just us and our family. We could hear the people in room 607 having an argument. And the people in room 609 had their television on so loudly it made our room buzz with the conversation. The people underneath us in room 508 were playing heavy-metal music and the floor bumped up and down with the beat. At least the sixth floor was the top floor, so there was no-one up above us making a racket.

'It's bedlam,' said Mum.

Bedlam is some old prison place where they put mad people, but it made me think of beds. I flopped down on to one of the single beds. It gave a creak and a groan. I didn't bounce a bit

43

on this bed. I just juddered to a halt. Bed number seven was a disappointment.

I tried the other single bed, just in case that was better. It was worse. The mattress sagged right down through the bedsprings. I set them all jangling as I jumped on.

'Elsa! Will you quit that!' Mack yelled.

'I was just trying out my bed, that's all. Sussing out where we're all going to sleep.' I decided to crack a bed joke to cheer us all up. 'Hey, where do baby apes sleep?'

'Give it a rest, Elsa, eh?' Mum sniffed.

'No, listen, it's good this one, really. Where do baby apes sleep? Can't you guess? Baby apes sleep in apricots.' I waited. They didn't even titter. '*Apricots*,' I said clearly, in case they hadn't got it first time round.

'Sh! Keep your voice down. Everyone can hear what you're saying,' said Mum.

'Then why isn't everybody laughing?' I said. 'Look, don't you get it? Baby apes . . .'

'That's *enough*!' Mack thundered. 'Button that lip.'

Honestly!

44

Then I had to unbutton, because I'd just thought of something.

'What about Hank? There isn't a bed for him,' I said.

We all looked round the room, as if a bed might suddenly appear out of nowhere.

'This will be Hank's little bedroom in here,' said Pippa, opening a cupboard door that stuck right out into the room, taking up even more of the space. It wasn't another bedroom. It was the shower and the loo and the washbasin, all cramped in together.

'We're going to be able to save time, you know. I reckon you could sit on the loo and clean your teeth and stick your feet in the shower all at the same time,' I said. 'Let's have a try, eh?'

'Look, come out of there, Elsa, and stop mucking about,' said Mum. 'This is ridiculous. Where *is* Hank going to sleep?'

'I'll go downstairs and tell them we're needing another bed,' said Mack.

'Yes, but where are we going to put it?' said Mum. 'There's no room to move as it is.'

'Maybe we'll have to take it in turns to move,' I said. 'You and Mack could stand in the shower while Pippa and Hank and I play for a bit, and then you could yell "All change" and we'll cram into the shower and you two could walk round and round the beds for a bit of exercise.'

I thought it an extremely sensible idea but they didn't think so.

'You'll be the one standing in the shower if you don't watch it,' said Mack. 'And the cold water will be on too.' He laughed. That's *his* idea of a joke.

He went all the way downstairs to tackle the big lady about another bed. Mum sat on the edge of the double bed, staring into space. Her eyes were watery again. She didn't notice when Hank got into her handbag and started licking her lipstick as if it was an ice lolly. I grabbed him and hauled him into the tiny shower space to mop him up a bit. The hot water tap in the basin was only lukewarm. I tried the shower to see if that had any hot. I couldn't work out how to switch it on. Pippa squeezed in too to give me a hand. I suddenly found the right knob to turn. I turned it a bit too far actually.

Mack's joke came true. It wasn't very funny. But at least we all got clean. Our clothes had a quick wash too. I dried us as best I could. I thought Mum might get mad but she didn't say a word. She just went on staring, as if she was looking right through the wall into room 607. They were still having their argument. It was getting louder. They were starting to use a lot of rude words.

'Um!' said Pippa, giggling.

Mack came storming back and he was mumbling a lot of rude words too. The hotel management didn't supply beds for children under two.

'Hank will have to go back in his cot,' he said, and he started piecing the bits of the old duck cot together again.

'But it's falling to bits now. And Hank's so big and bouncy. He kept thumping and jumping last time he was in it. He'll smash it up in seconds,' I said.

'And that's not Hank's cot any more. It's my Baby Pillow's bed,' said Pippa indignantly.

'Baby Pillow will have to sleep with you, my wee chook,' said Mack.

'But he won't like that. Baby Pillow will cry and kick me,' said Pippa.

'Well, you'll just have to cry and kick him back,' said Mack, reaching out and giving her

47

a little poke in the tummy. He noticed her T-shirt was a little damp.

'Here, how come you're soaking wet?' said Mack, frowning.

I held my breath. If Pippa told on me I wouldn't half be for it. Yes, for it. And five it and six it too.

But Pippa was a pal. She just mumbled something about splashing herself, so Mack grunted and got on with erecting the duck cot for Hank. I gratefully helped Pippa find Baby Pillow and all his things from one of the black plastic rubbish bags we'd carted from our old house.

My sister Pippa is crackers. Mack was always buying her dolls when he was in work and we were rich. All the different Barbies, My Little Ponies, those big special dolls that walk and talk and wet, but Pippa's only ever wanted Baby Pillow. Baby Pillow got born when Mum had Hank. Pippa started carting this old pillow round with her, talking to it and rocking it as if it were a baby. He's rather a backward baby if he's as old as Hank, because he hasn't started crawling yet. If I'm feeling in a very good mood I help Pippa feed Baby Pillow with one of Hank's old bottles and we change his old nappy and bundle him up into an old nightie and then we tuck him up in the duck cot and tell him to go to sleep. I generally make him cry quite a bit first and Pippa has to keep rocking him and telling him stories.

'We won't be able to play our game if Hank's got to go in the duck cot,' Pippa grumbled.

But when Mack had got the cot standing in the last available spot of space and we tried stuffing Hank into his old baby bed, Hank himself decided this just wasn't on. He howled indignantly and started rocking the bars and cocking his leg up, trying to escape.

'He'll have that over in no time,' said Mack. 'So what are we going to do, eh?'

He looked over at Mum. She was still staring into space. She was acting as if she couldn't hear Mack or even Hank's bawling.

'Mum?' said Pippa, and she clutched Baby Pillow anxiously.

'Hey, Mum,' I said, and I went and shook her shoulder. She wasn't crying any more. This was worse. She didn't even take any notice of me.

'Here,' said Mack, grabbing Hank, hauling him out of the cot and dumping him into Mum's lap.

For a moment Mum kept her arms limply by her side, her face still blank. Hank howled harder, hurt that he was getting ignored. He raised his arms, wanting a hug. He stretched higher, lost his balance, and nearly toppled right off Mum's lap and on to the floor. But just in time Mum's hands grabbed him and pulled him close against her chest.

'Don't cry. I've got you,' said Mum, sighing. She blinked, back in herself again.

'Where's the wee boy going to sleep, then?' Mack asked again.

Mum shrugged.

'He'll have to sleep with one of his sisters, won't he,' she said.

'Not me!' I said quickly.

'Not me either,' said Pippa. 'He wets right out of his nappies.'

Hank went on crying.

'He's hungry,' said Mum. 'We could all do with a drink and a bite to eat. I'm going to go and find this communal kitchen. Here Hank, go to Daddy. And you girls, you get all our stuff unpacked from those bags, right?'

Yes, everything was all right again. Mum rolled up her sleeves and got the cardboard box with our kettle and our pots and pans and some tins of food and went off to find the kitchen. Mack romped on the bed with Hank, and he stopped crying and started chuckling. Pippa said Baby Pillow was still crying though, and she insisted she had to tuck him up in the duck cot and put him to sleep.

So I got lumbered doing most of the unpacking. There were two bags full of Pippa's clothes and Hank's baby stuff. There was an old suitcase stuffed with Mum and Mack's clothes and Mum's hairdryer and her make-up and her precious china crinoline lady. And there was my carrier bag. I don't have that many clothes because I always get them mucked up anyway. I've got T-shirts and shorts for the summer, and jumpers and jeans for the winter, and some knickers and socks and stuff. I've got a

Minnie Mouse hairbrush though it doesn't ever get all the tangles out of my mane of hair. I've got a green marble that I used to pretend was magic. I've got my box of felt-tip pens. Most of the colours have run out and Pippa mucked up some of the points when she was little, but I don't feel like throwing them away yet. Sometimes I colour a ghost picture, pretending the colours in my head. Then there are my joke books. They are a bit torn and tatty

because I thumb through them so often.

I hoped Mum would be ever so pleased with me getting all our stuff sorted out and the room all neat and tidy but she came back so flaming mad she hardly noticed.

'This is ridiculous,' she said, dumping the cardboard box so violently that all the pots and pans played a tune. 'I had to queue up for ages just to get into this crummy little kitchen, and then when some of these other women were finished and I got my chance, I realized that it was all a waste of time anyway. You should see the state of that stove! It's filthy. I'd have to scrub at it for a week before I'd set my saucepans on it. Even the floor's so slimy with grease I nearly slipped and fell. What are we going to do, Mack?'

'You're asking Big Mack, right?' said Mack, throwing Hank up in the air so he shrieked with delight. 'Big Mack says let's go and eat Big Macs at McDonald's.'

Pippa and I shrieked with delight too. Mum didn't look so thrilled.

'And what are we going to live on for the rest of the week, eh?' she said. 'We can't eat out all the time, Mack.'

'Come on now, hen, give it a rest. You just now said we can't eat in. So we'll eat out today. Tomorrow will just have to take care of itself.'

'The sun will come out tooomorrow . . .' I sang. I maybe don't have a very sweet voice but it is strong.

'Elsa! Keep your voice down!' Mum hissed.

Mack pulled a silly face and covered up his ears, pretending to be deafened.

We sang the Tomorrow song at school. It comes from a musical about a little orphan girl called Annie. Occasionally I think I'd rather like to be Little Orphan Elsa.

Still, I cheered up considerably because McDonald's is one of my all-time favourite places. Mum changed Hank and we all got ready to go out. It was odd using the little loo in the bedroom. Pippa didn't like it with everybody listening so I trekked down the corridor with her to find a proper ladies' toilet. If Mum saw it she'd get flaming mad again. Pippa got even more upset, hopping about agitatedly, so I ended up trailing her down six flights of stairs and down the corridor to the toilet where we met Naomi. I hoped she might still be there, but she'd gone. The boys weren't hanging around any more either. The rude words were still on the wall though.

We'd worked up quite an appetite by the time we'd trudged up the stairs to put on our jumpers and then down all over again with Mum and Mack and Hank. It was a long long walk into the town to find the McDonald's too. Pippa started to lag behind and Mum kept twisting her ankle in her high heels. I started to get a bit tired too, and my toes rubbed up against the edge of my trainers because they're getting too small for me. Mum moaned about being stuck in a dump of a hotel at the back of beyond and said she couldn't walk another step. Mack stopped at a phone box and said he'd call a cab then, and Mum said he was crazy and it was no wonder we'd all ended up in bed and breakfast.

It was starting to sound like a very big row. I was getting scared that we'd maybe end up with no tea at all. But then we got to a bus stop and a bus came along and we all climbed on and we were in the town in no time. At McDonald's.

Mack had his Big Mac. Mum had chicken nuggets. I chose a cheeseburger and Pippa did too because she always copies me. Hank nibbled his own French fries and experienced his very first strawberry milkshake.

It was great. We didn't have a big row. We didn't even have a little one. We sat in the warm, feeling full, and Mack pulled Pippa on to his lap and Mum put her arm round me, and Hank nodded off in his buggy still clutching a handful of chips.

We looked like an ordinary happy family having a meal out. But we didn't go back to an ordinary happy family house. We had to go back to the Bed-and-Breakfast hotel.

The people in 607 were still arguing. The people in 609 still had their television blaring. The people in 508 were still into heavy-metal music. And it was even more of a squash in room 608.

We all went to bed because there wasn't much else to do. Mum and Mack in the double bed. Pippa and Hank either end of one single bed. Me in the other. Baby Pillow the comfiest of the lot in the duck cot.

Hank wasn't the only one who wet in the night. Pippa did too, so she had to creep in with me. She went back to sleep straightaway, but I didn't. I wriggled around uncomfortably, Pippa's hair tickling my nose and her elbow digging into my chest. I stared up into the dark while Mack snored and Hank snuffled and I wished I could rise out of my crowded bed, right through the roof and up into the starry sky.

We've always had different breakfasts. Mum's never really bothered. She just likes a cup of coffee and a ciggie. She says she can't fancy food early in the morning. She cooks for Mack though. He likes great greasy bacon sandwiches and a cup of strong tea with four sugars. I'd like four sugars in my tea but Mum won't let me. It's not fair. She does sometimes let me have a sugar sandwich for my breakfast though, if she's in a very good mood. I say *she* needs to eat a sugar sandwich to sweeten herself up.

Pippa likes sugar sandwiches too, because she always copies me. Hank has a runny boiled egg that certainly runs all over him. His face is

57

bright yellow by the time he's finished his breakfast, and he always insists on clutching his buttered toast soldiers until he's squeezed them into a soggy pulp. Sometimes I can see why Mum can't face food herself. Mopping up my baby brother would put anyone off their breakfast.

Mum certainly didn't look like she wanted any breakfast our first morning at the Royal. She'd obviously tossed and turned a lot in the night because her hair was all sticking up at the back. Her eyes looked red and sore. I'd heard her crying in the night.

'How about you taking the kids down to breakfast, Mack?' she said pleadingly. 'I don't think I could face it today. I'm feeling ever so queasy.'

'Aw, come on, hen. I can't cope with all three of them on my own. I'm not Mary Piddly Poppins.'

'You don't have to cope with me,' I said indignantly.

'I sometimes wish to God I didn't,' Mack growled.

He's always like that with me. Ready to bite my head off. He's the one who's like a lion, not me.

I wish I could figure out some way of taming him.

'I'll feed Hank for you, Mum, and see that Pippa has a proper breakfast,' I promised kindly.

'Your mum's going to have a proper breakfast herself,' said Mack. 'That's what she needs to make her feel better. A good cooked breakfast. And if we're getting it as part of this lousy bed-and-breakfast deal then we ought to make sure we all eat every last mouthful.'

'All right, I'm coming,' said Mum, slapping a

bit of make-up on her pale face and fiddling with her hair. She took out her mirror from her handbag and winced. 'I look a right sight,' she wailed.

'You look fine to me,' said Mack, giving her powdered cheek a kiss. 'And you'll look even better once you've got a fried egg and a few rashers of bacon inside you.'

'Don't, Mack! You're going to make me throw up,' said Mum.

I'd throw up if Mack started slobbering at me like that.

We trailed down all the stairs to the ground floor, where this breakfast room was supposed to be. Mack started sniffing, his hairy nostrils all aquiver.

'Can't smell any bacon sizzling,' he said.

We soon found out why. There wasn't any bacon for breakfast. There wasn't very much of anything. Just pots of tea and bowls of corn-flakes and slices of bread, very white and very square, like the ceiling tiles in reception. You just went and served yourself and sat at one of the tables.

'No bacon?' said Mack, and he stormed off to the reception desk.

'Hank needs his egg,' said Mum, and she marched off after Mack, Hank balanced on her hip.

Pippa and I sighed and shrugged our shoulders. We straggled off after them.

The big lady was behind the desk. She was wearing a fluffy blue jumper this time. I hoped she'd painted her fingernails blue to match, but she hadn't. Still, Mack was certainly turning the air blue, shouting and swearing because there weren't any cooked breakfasts.

'It's your duty to provide a proper breakfast. They said so down at the Social. I'm going to report you,' Mack thundered.

'We don't have any duty whatsoever, sir. If you don't care to stay at the Royal Hotel then why don't you leave?' said the big lady.

'You know very well we can't leave, because we haven't got anywhere else to go. And it's a disgrace. My kids need a good breakfast – my baby boy needs his protein or he'll get ill,' said Mum.

She spoke as if Hank was on the point of starving right this minute, although she was sagging sideways trying to support her strapping great son. He was reaching longingly for this new blue bunny.

The big lady stepped backwards, away from his sticky clasp.

'We're providing extra milk for all the children at the moment. We normally do provide a full cooked breakfast but unfortunately we are temporarily between breakfast chefs, so in these circumstances we can only offer a continental breakfast. Take it – or leave it.'

We decided to take it.

'Continental breakfast!' said Mum, as we sat at a table in the corner. 'That's coffee in one of them cafetière thingys and croissants, not this sort of rubbish.' She flapped one of the limp slices of bread in the air. 'There's no goodness in this!'

There were little packets of butter and pots of marmalade. And sugar lumps. Lots of sugar lumps.

I got busy crushing and sprinkling. I made myself a splendid sugar sandwich. Pippa tried to make herself one too, but she wasn't much good at crushing the lumps. She tried bashing them hard on the table to make them shatter.

'Pippa! Give over, for goodness sake. Whatever are you doing?' said Mum, spooning cornflakes into Hank.

'It's Elsa's fault. Pippa's just copying her,' said Mack. 'Here, give me that sugar bowl and stop messing around. You'll rot your teeth and just have empty gums by the time you're twelve.'

I covered my teeth with my lips and made little gulpy noises to see what it would be like. I tried sucking at my sandwich to see if I'd still be able to eat without teeth. I swallowed before the lump in my mouth got soft enough, and choked.

'Elsa! Look, do you have to show us all up?' Mum hissed.

'Stop it!' said Mack. 'Otherwise you'll get a good smacking, see?'

I saw. I was trying like anything to stop choking. I got up, coughing and spluttering, and went over to the service hatch to get myself some more milk. There was a big black lady with a baby serving herself. I wondered if she might be Naomi's mum and asked her between coughs.

She said she wasn't, but helpfully banged me on the back. I took a long drink of milk and peered all round the room, hoping to spot Naomi. There were old people and young people and lots of little kids, black people and white people and brown people and yellow people, quiet people and noisy people and absolutely bawling babies. But I couldn't spot Naomi anywhere. Maybe she had her breakfast sitting in the washbasin in the Ladies.

I did spot one of the boys who'd been writing rude words all over the wall. He saw me looking at him and crossed his eyes and stuck out his tongue. I did likewise.

'Elsa!' Mum came and yanked me back to our table. 'Don't you dare make faces like that.'

I pulled another face, because I was getting fed up with everyone picking on me when it wasn't my fault. Then I saw a lovely lady with lots of little plaits come into the breakfast room. She had two little boys with her, and she was carrying a toddler. And there was a girl following on behind, her head in a book.

'NAOMI!' I yelled excitedly, jumping up.

Mack was taking a large gulp of tea at that precise second. Somehow or other the tea sprayed all down his front. He didn't look too happy. I decided to dash over to Naomi pretty sharpish.

'Hi, Naomi. I've been looking out for you. Is this your mum? Are these your brothers?'

I said hello to them all and they smiled and said hello back.

'Is that your dad over there? That man shouting at you,' said Naomi.

'No fear,' I said. 'What are you reading then, eh?'

I had a quick peer. The cover said *Little Women* and there was a picture of four girls in old-fashioned frocks.

'*Little Women?*' I said, thinking it a rather naff title.

'It's a lovely book, one of the classics,' said Naomi's mum proudly. 'My Naomi's always reading it.'

'Boring,' I mumbled, peering at the pages.

'The Cursed Werewolf seized the young maiden and ripped her to pieces with his huge yellow teeth. . .'

'There's a werewolf in *Little Women*?' I said, astonished.

'Sh!' said Naomi, giving me a nudge. She turned her back so that her mum couldn't see and quickly lifted the dustjacket off *Little Women*. She had a different book entirely underneath. *The Cursed Werewolf Runs Wild*.

'Ah,' I said. I decided I liked Naomi even more.

I sat down at their table, even though Mack was bellowing fit to bust for me to come back at once OR ELSE. Naomi's little brothers looked utterly angelic above the table, all big eyes and smiley mouths, but they were conducting a violent kicking match out of sight. One of the kicks landed right on my kneecap. I gave a little scream and both boys looked anxiously at their mum. I didn't tell tales, but I seized hold of several skinny legs and tickled unmercifully. They squirmed and doubled up.

'Boys!' said Naomi's mum. 'Stop messing about.'

She was trying to feed the baby but he kept fidgeting and turning his head away, not wanting his soggy old cornflakes.

'Come on, Nathan,' said Naomi's mum.

Nathan shut his mouth tight and let cornflake mush dribble down his chin.

'How about feeding him like an aeroplane?' I suggested. 'My baby brother Hank likes it when I do that. Here, I'll show you.'

I took the spoon, filled it with flakes, and then let my arm zoom through the air above Nathan's head.

'Here's a loaded jumbo jet coming in to land,' I said and made very loud aeroplane noises.

Nathan opened his mouth in astonishment and I shoved the spoon in quick.

'Unloading bay in operation,' I said, and I unhooked the empty spoon from his gums.

'Come on then, Nathan, gobble gobble, while I go looking for the next aeroplane. Hey, how about a Concorde this time?'

Nathan chewed obediently while I reloaded the spoon and held it at the right Concorde angle. I revved up my sound system.

Unfortunately, my dear non-relative Uncle Mack was revving up his own sound system. After one last bellow he came charging like a bull across the breakfast room.

I landed Concorde, unloaded the new cargo of cornflakes inside Nathan, and tried turning the spoon into a bomber plane with mega-quick, whizz-bang missiles.

Mack certainly exploded. But not in the way I wanted.

'How dare you make this ridiculous noise and bother these poor people,' he roared, yanking me up from the table.

'Oh no, she's been no bother at all,' said Naomi's mum quickly. 'So Elsa's your daughter, is she?'

'No!' I said.

'No!' Mack said.

It was about the only thing we ever agreed on.

'Elsa is my stepdaughter,' said Mack. He said the word 'step' as if it was some disgusting swear word. 'I've done my best to bring her up as if she was my own, but she gets right out of hand sometimes.'

I wished I was out of his hand at that precise moment. He was holding me by the shoulders, his fingers digging in hard.

'Well, she's been a very good girl with us, helping me keep my family in order,' said Naomi's mum.

'Yes, she got my baby brother Nathan to eat up all his cornflakes,' said Naomi.

'It's a pity she can't help out with her own brother and sister then,' said Mack. 'Come on, Elsa, your mum needs you.'

He gave a jerk and a pull. I had to go with him or else get my arm torn off. I looked back at Naomi.

'The Cursed Werewolf!' I mouthed, nodding at Mack.

Naomi nodded, grinning at me sympathetically.

I needed sympathy. Mack was in a foul mood.

'What do you think you're doing, rushing

around yelling your head off?' he yelled, rushing around.

I could sense it wasn't quite the right time to point out that I was only following my step-daddy's example. He got me sat back at our table and started giving me this right old lecture about learning to do as I was told. Pippa started fidgeting and shifting about on her chair as if she were the one getting the lecture, not me.

'I'm needing to go to the toilet,' she announced.

'Well, off you go then,' said Mack.

'I can't find it by myself,' said Pippa.

'I'll take her,' I said, jumping at the chance.

I clutched Pippa's hand and escaped the Werewolf's copious curses. Some of the boys were back down the corridor, writing more rude words on the walls. An old lady with a hoover rounded a corner and saw what they were up to.

'Here, you clean that off, you little var-mints,' she yelled, aiming her vacuum at them.

They laughed and said the words to her.

'Dirty beasts,' said the hoover lady.

She saw us gawping.

'Cover your ears up, girls. And you'd better close your eyes too. These little whatsits are

71

desecrating this hotel. Blooming desecrating it, that's what they are.' She banged up against the boys with the vacuum, running the suction nozzle up and down the nearest's shell suit.

'Get off, will you! My mum's only just bought me this,' he yelled indignantly.

'I'm just trying to clean you up, laddie. Get some of the dirt off you. Now clear off, the lot of you, or I'll fetch the Manager.'

They straggled away while she held her vacuum aloft in victory. Pippa and I giggled. Mrs Hoover followed us into the Ladies so she could have a quick smoke.

'Dear oh dear, this place will be the death of me,' she said, lighting up. She tucked her ciggies and matches back in her pocket and flexed her legs in her baggy old trousers. 'It used to be a really classy establishment back in the old days. A really nice business hotel. You could get fantastic tips and everyone spoke to you ever so pleasant. Now you just get a mouthful of abuse. They're all scum that stay here now. Absolute scum.'

She said this very fiercely and then blinked a bit at me.

'No offence meant, dearie. You seem very nice little girls, you and your sister.'

'Are we just a bit scummy round the edges then?' I said.

'You what? Oh, give over!' She drew on her cigarette, chuckling.

'What's scum?' said Pippa, emerging from the toilet and going to wash her hands.

'That's scum,' I said, wiping my finger round the edge of the grey basin.

'Now dear, don't shame me. I used to keep this place so clean you could eat your dinner out of one of them basins. But now I just lose heart. And the management's so mean, they keep cutting down the staff. How can I keep all this place spick and span, eh, especially with my legs.' She patted at her trousers and shook

73

her head. Then she had another glance at the basin. 'Look, that's a footprint, isn't it? Dear goodness, would you credit it? They're actually putting their feet in the basins now.'

'I wonder who on earth that could be,' I said, winking at Pippa.

'I know!' said Pippa, not understanding my meaningful wink.

'No you don't,' I said quickly. 'Here, we could help you do a bit of the cleaning if you like, Pippa and me. I'm good at vacuuming. It's fun.'

I wasn't in any hurry to get back to the breakfast room and Mack. I wanted him to cool down a bit first. So Mrs Hoover sat stiffly on the stairs and did a bit of dusting and Pippa pottered about with a dustpan and brush while I switched on the vacuum and sucked up all the dust on the shabby carpet.

I kept imagining Mack was standing right in front of me. I'd charge at him and knock him flying and then get out a really giant suction nozzle. I wouldn't just snag his shell suit, *oh* no. I'd hoover him right out of existence.

I was galloping along the corridor, laughing fit to bust, when the real Mack suddenly came round the corner. He didn't look very cool at all. He looked as if he might very well be at boiling point.

'What the heck are you playing at, Elsa?'

'I'm not playing, I'm helping do the housework.'

'Switch it off! And don't answer me back like that,' Mack said. 'We thought you'd both got lost. You've been gone nearly half an hour. Didn't you realize you'd be worrying your mum? Elsa!'

'I thought you didn't want me to answer you,' I said.

Mack took a step nearer to me, breathing fire.

'Don't be cross with the kiddie, she's been ever such a help,' said Mrs Hoover. 'She's got this carpet up a treat, I'm telling you. And the little one's been sweeping the stairs, haven't you, pet?'

'Yes, well, I'll thank you to mind your own business,' said Mack, snatching Pippa up into his arms. 'You come with Daddy, chook. We've been worried sick, wondering what had happened to you.

Mum's been right up to our room and back, thinking you'd gone up there.'

Mack stomped round the corner, still clutching Pippa, and tripped right over the gang of giggling boys writing more dirty words on the wall.

'Get out of my way, you kids,' Mack thundered.

Pippa peered at the words from her new vantage point. She stared at the worst word of all. She remembered. She said it loudly and clearly.

'What did you say, Pippa?' said Mack, so taken aback he nearly dropped her.

So she said it again. Unmistakably.

'I'm reading, Dad,' she said proudly.

The boys absolutely cracked up at this, sniggering and spluttering.

'I'll wipe the smile off your silly faces!' Mack shouted, practically frothing at the mouth. 'How dare you write mucky words on the wall so that my little girl learns dirt like that?'

They stopped sniggering and started scattering, seeing that Mack meant business. Mack caught hold of one of them, the boy I'd made the face at. He was pulling faces again now, trying to wriggle free.

'It wasn't me that wrote that word, honest!' he yelled. 'It was her.'

He pointed to me. All his pals stopped and pointed to me too.

'Yes, it was that girl.'

'Yes, that one with all the hair.'

'Yeah, that little girl with the loud voice.'

It looked like I was in BIG TROUBLE.

I was.

I tried to explain but Mack wouldn't listen.

He hit. And I hurt.

Sweets for Treats

Mack stayed in a horrible mood all that day. All that *week*. And Mum wasn't much better. She didn't get mad at me and shout. She didn't say very much at all. She did a lot of that sitting on the bed and staring into space. Sometimes Mack could snap her out of it. Sometimes he couldn't.

I hated to see Mum all sad and sulky like that. I tried telling her jokes to cheer her up a bit.

'Hey Mum, what's ten metres tall and green and sits in the corner?'

'Oh Elsa, please. Just leave me be.'

'The Incredible Sulk!'

I fell about. But Mum didn't even smile.

'OK, try this one. Why did the biscuit cry?'

'What biscuit? What are you on about?'

'Any biscuit.'

'Can I have a biscuit, Mum?' said Pippa.

'Look, just listen to the *joke*. Why did the biscuit cry, eh? Because his mother was a wafer so long.'

I paused. Nobody reacted.

'Don't you get it?'

'Just give it a rest, Elsa, please,' Mum said, and she lay back on her bed and buried her head under the pillow.

I stared at Mum worriedly. I so badly wanted her to cheer up.

'Mum? Mum.' I went over to her and shook her arm.

'Leave her be,' said Mack.

I took no notice.

'Mum, what happened to the lady who slept with her head under the pillow?'

Mum groaned.

'When she woke up she found the fairies had taken all her teeth out!'

Mum didn't twitch.

'Elsa, I'm telling you. Leave her alone,' Mack growled.

I tried just one more.

'Are you going to sleep, Mum? Listen, what happened to the lady who dreamed she was eating a huge great marshmallow?'

'Can I have a marshmallow?' said Pippa.

'When she woke up her pillow had disappeared!'

Mum didn't move. But Mack did.

'I'm warning you, Elsa. Just one more of your stupid jokes and you're for it!'

'Dad, can I have some biscuits or some sweets or something? I'm hungry,' Pippa whined.

'OK, OK.' Mack fumbled in his pocket for change. 'Take her down to that shop on the corner, Elsa. Here.'

'What do Eskimos use for money? Ice lolly!'

'I thought I told you. NO MORE JOKES!'

'OK, OK.' I grabbed Pippa and scooted out the room.

'Why are adults boring?' I asked her, as we went down the stairs. 'Because they're groan-ups.'

I roared with laughter. I'm not altogether sure Pippa understood, but she laughed too to keep me company. The big bunny lady in reception put her pointy finger to her lips and went 'Sh! Sh!' at us.

'She sounds like a train,' I said to Pippa. 'Hey, what do you call a train full of toffee?'

'Oh, toffee! Are you buying toffee? I like toffee too.'

'No, Pippa, you're not concentrating. What do you call a train full of toffee? A chew-chew train.'

Pippa blinked up at me blankly. I laughed. She laughed too, but she was just copying me like she always does. I wished she was old enough to appreciate my jokes. I longed to try them all out on Naomi, but she was at school.

That was one of the advantages of going to live at the O Yal Htl. I couldn't go to my old school because it was miles and miles away. No-one had said anything about going to any other school. I certainly wasn't going to bring the subject up.

I took hold of Pippa's hand and we went out of the hotel and down the road to where there was this one shop selling sweets and ciggies and papers and videos – all the things you need.

Some of the boys from the hotel were mucking around at the video stands, whizzing them round too fast and acting out bits from the films. One of them lunged at me with his hands all pointy, pretending to be Freddie from Elm Street.

'Ooooh, I'm so fwightened,' I said, sighing heavily. 'What are you lot doing here, anyway? Are you bunking off from school?'

They shuffled a bit so I was obviously right.

'Don't you tell on us or you'll get it, see,' said another, trying to act dead tough.

'Don't worry. *I* don't tell tales,' I said, looking witheringly at the funny-face boy who had told on me.

He shuffled a bit more, his face going red.

'Yeah, well, I didn't think your dad would get mad at you like that,' he said quickly.

'He's not my dad. He's just my mum's bloke, that's all.'

'Did he hit you? We heard you yelling.'

'You'd yell if he was laying into you.'

'Here. Have this,' said the funny-face boy, and he handed me his big black magic-marker pen, the one I'd used to correct his spelling to write the truly worst word ever.

'Hey, are you giving this to me?' I said.

'Yeah, if you want.'

'You bet I want! My own black felt-tip's run out. Hey, what goes black and white, black and white, black and white?'

'Hmm?' he said, looking blank.

But one of his mates spoilt it.

'A nun rolling down a hill,' he said, grinning. 'That's an *old* joke.'

'OK, OK, what's black and white and goes ha-ha?'

I paused. This time I'd got them.

'The nun that pushed her!'

Funny-face suddenly snorted with laughter. The others all sniggered too. Laughing at my joke! I'd have happily stood there cracking jokes all day but the man behind the counter started to get narked so the boys sloped off while Pippa and I chose our sweets. It took a long time, especially as Pippa kept chopping and changing. Once or twice she changed her mind *after* she'd had a little experimental lick of a liquorice bootlace or a red jelly spider, but the man behind the counter couldn't see down far enough to spot her.

We ended up with:

We ate them on the way back to the hotel. We weren't in any hurry to get back. Mack had been so grouchy recently he'd even got mad at Pippa.

I meant to save a chocolate bar for Naomi, and a toffee chew or two for her brothers, but I seemed to get ever so hungry somehow, and by the time Naomi got back from school there were just a few dolly mixtures left (and they were a bit dusty and sticky because Pippa had been 'feeding' them to Baby Pillow half the afternoon).

'Never mind, I'll give them a little wash under the tap,' said Naomi, going into the Ladies.

She and I scrunched up together on the windowsill, feet propped on the basin, and we read the worst bits of her Cursed Werewolf book and got the giggles. My Pippa and her Nicky and Neil and Nathan kept on plaguing us so we filled the other basins with water and hauled them up so they could have a little paddle. They were only meant to dangle their feet. They dangled quite a bit more.

I was scared I'd get into trouble with Mum and Mack for getting Pippa soaked, but luckily Mum didn't notice and Mack had gone out for a takeaway and taken Hank with him. Hank loves to go anywhere with Mack. He's a really weird baby. He thinks his dad is great.

I think Mack is great too. A great big hairy warthog.

Pippa and Nicky and Neil and Nathan weren't the only ones who got soaked when they went paddling in the basins. The floor in the Ladies turned into a sort of sea too. Naomi and I tried to mop it up a bit but we only had loo paper to do it with so we weren't very successful.

Mrs Hoover had to mop it up properly and she wasn't very pleased. I felt bad about it so the next day Pippa and I helped her with her hoovering. I'd got lumbered with Hank as well, but I tried hard to get him to flick a duster. He seemed determined to use it as a cuddle blanket but Mrs Hoover didn't mind.

'Oh, what a little sweetie! Bless him!' she cooed.

'Have you got some sweeties?' Pippa asked hopefully.

'You're just like my little granddaughter, pet. Always on at her Nan for sweeties. Here you are, then.' Mrs Hoover gave us both a fruit drop. Hank had to make do with chewing his duster, because he might swallow the fruit drop whole and choke.

'Yum yum, I've got an orange. I nearly like them best. I like the red bestest of all,' said Pippa hopefully.

I tutted at her but Mrs Hoover tittered.

'You're a greedy little madam,' she said, handing over a raspberry drop too.

'What do you say, Pippa, eh?' I said.

'Thank you ever so much Mrs Hoover.'

'You what?' said Mrs Hoover, because Mrs Hoover wasn't her real name at all, it was just our name for her. Her real name was Mrs Macpherson but I didn't like calling her that because it reminded me too much of my Mack Person. My least favourite person of all time.

He'd given me another smack because Pippa and I were playing hunt the magic marble in our room and I'd hidden it under the rug covering the torn part of the carpet. How was I to know that Mack would burst back from the betting shop and stomp across the rug and skid on the marble and go flying?

I couldn't help laughing. He really did look hilarious. Especially when he landed bonk on his bum.

'I'll teach you not to laugh at me!' he said, scrabbling up.

He did his best.

But I've had the last laugh. I sloped off into the Ladies all by myself and had a little fun with my new black magic-marker pen.

Mega-Feast for Lunch

I soon got into a Royal Hotel routine. I always woke up early. I'd scrunch up in bed with my torch and my joke books and wise up on a few more wisecracks. I'd tell the jokes over and over until I had them off by heart. I'd often roll around laughing myself.

Sometimes I shook the bed so much Pippa woke up wondering if she was in the middle of an earthquake. If I caused earthquakes Pippa was liable to cause her own natural disasters. Floods.

Mum kept getting mad at her and saying she was much too big to be wetting the bed and she didn't let Pippa have anything to drink at teatime but it still didn't make much difference. Pippa cried because she was so thirsty and she *still* wet the bed more often than not.

So another of my little routines was to sneak all Pippa's wet bedclothes down to the laundry room before Mum and Mack woke up. There were only two washing machines and one dryer. You usually couldn't get near them. But early in the morning everyone was either fast asleep or getting the kids ready for school so there was a good chance I could wash the sheets out for my leaky little sister.

The only other people around were some of the Asian ladies in their pretty clothes. They looked like people out of fairy tales instead of ordinary mums in boring old T-shirts and leggings. They sounded as if they were saying strange and secret things too as they whispered together in their own language. Some of their children could speak good English even though they'd only been over here a few months, but the mums didn't bother. They generally just stuck in a little clump together.

I felt a bit shy of them at first and I think they felt shy with me too. But after a few encounters in the laundry room we started to nod to each other. One time they'd run out of washing powder so I gave them a few sprinkles of ours. The next day they gave me half a packet back *and* a special pink sweet. It was the sweetest sweet I'd ever eaten in my life. It was so sweet it started to get sickly, and when I got back to room 608 I passed it on to Pippa. She enjoyed it hugely for a while but it finally got the better of her too. We rubbed a little on Hank's dummy and it kept him quiet half the morning.

Keeping Hank quiet was a task and a half at the hotel. He'd always been a happy sort of baby, even if he did act like a bit of a thug at times, bashing about with his fat fists and kicking hard with his bootees. But he'd never really whined and whimpered that much. Now he didn't seem to do much else. It was probably because he was so cooped up. He was just getting to the stage when he wanted to crawl around all over the place and explore. But he couldn't really crawl in room 608. It was much too little and crowded.

It was dangerous too. If you took your eye off him for two seconds he'd be doing this

or this

or this.

There was only one way to keep him out of mischief.

He didn't like it one little bit. He wanted to be up and about.

Mum and Mack didn't want to be up and about at all. They just wanted to sleep in. Most days they even stopped bothering to go down to breakfast. So Pippa and Hank and I had our breakfast and then we helped Mrs Hoover and then we played about in the corridor. We set Hank down at one end and charged up to the other end and had a very quick game before he caught up with us.

Hank got so good at crawling he could probably win a gold medal at the Baby Olympics. If we wanted any peace at all we had to change his crawling track into an obstacle race.

Sometimes we collected several babies and had a proper race. The other brothers and sisters placed bets. That was good. Pippa and I coined it in, because Hank always won.

We got a bit noisy and sometimes Mack would come staggering out into the corridor and tell us all to pipe down. He'd yell if he was in a bad mood but he didn't frighten anyone now. The kids just muttered amongst themselves about pimply bums and brain transplants and cracked up laughing. All the girls had read the jokes in the Ladies toilet downstairs. Even some of the boys had dashed in and out for a dare.

Mack and Mum often didn't get up properly until lunchtime. Lunch was my favourite meal of the day because I could nip along to the shop on the corner and choose it. I had to make sure I bought a packet of ciggies for Mum and the *Sun* for Mack, and maybe something boring like a carton of milk or a packet of biscuits –

but then I could buy crisps and Coke and chocolates and sweets and anything else I fancied with the money left over. Pippa and I always had a Mega-Feast.

SAMPLE WEEK'S MENU OF THE MEGA-FEAST

Monday:	Apple juice, Mini Cheddars, Toffee Crisp, Woppa, Spearmint chew
Tuesday:	Strawberry Ribena, Californian corn chips, Cadbury's Flake, Buster bar
Wednesday:	Lucozade, Chicken Tikka Hula Hoops, Bounty, Flying Saucers
Thursday:	Dr Pepper drink, Chipsticks, Galaxy, Sherbert Fountain
Friday:	Coke, Salt-and-vinegar crisps, Crunchie, Fizz cola-bottle sweets
Saturday:	Strawberry Break Time Milk, Pork scratchings, Picnic, Dolly-beads
Sunday:	Lilt, Skips (chilli flavour), Fruit-and-nut chocolate, Giant Bootlace

This is all times two, because Pippa always copied me. Hank generally wanted a lick here and a munch there after he'd had his bottle and his baby tins, but there was still heaps left for us.

We sometimes went out in the afternoons. Once we went to the park.

I liked it best of all when Mack went down the betting shop and took Hank along too and Mum and Pippa and me went to the shops. Not the shop on the corner. Not the Kwik-Save or the off-licence or the chip shop down the road. The real shops in the town. Especially the

Flowerfields Shopping Centre. It's this great glass shopping mall with real flowers blossoming in big bouquets all round the entrance, and painted flowers spiralling over the door of each individual shop, and there are lovely ladies wandering round in long dresses who hand you a flower for free.

Mum and Pippa and I could spend hours and hours and hours wandering round the Flowerfields Shopping Centre.

Of course we couldn't ever buy the books or the tapes or the toys or the outfits. But we could go back the next day and the next and read and listen and play and try them on all over again. And then when we had to trail all the way back to the Oyal Htl and we were all tired and we didn't even have the money for the bus, we could still smell our flowers and pretend they were big bouquets.

I made up this story to myself that I was a famous comedienne and I'd just done this amazingly funny routine on stage and everyone had laughed and laughed and then they'd clapped and clapped and begged for an encore and showered me with roses . . .

'Hey, Mum, Pippa, what do you get if you cross a rose with a python?'

'Oh Elsa, please, give it a rest.'

'I don't know what you get – but don't try to smell it!' I laughed. Then I tried again.

'What did one rose say to the other rose?'

'Hello, Rose,' said Pippa. She laughed. 'Hey, I said the joke!'

'Don't you start too,' Mum groaned.

'That's not a joke, Pippa. It's not funny. No, *listen*. What did one rose say to the other rose? It said . . . Hi, Bud. See? *That's* funny.'

'No it's not,' said Mum.

I ignored her.

'All right then. What did the bee say to the flower?'

'Hi, flower?' said Pippa. 'Is that right? Have I said the joke now?'

'No! Pippa, you can't just say any old thing. It's got to be a joke. Now, what did the bee say to the flower? It said, Hello honey.'

'And I'm going to say Goodbye Sweetie if you dare come out with one more of your daft jokes,' said Mum, but she didn't really mean it. She was just joking herself.

Mum could still be a lot of fun, especially going round Flowerfields – but when we got back to room 608 she wilted like the flowers.

We spent the evenings indoors. So did everyone else around us. The people in room 607 had more arguments. The people in room 609 still had their telly blaring. The people underneath in room 508 still played their heavy-metal music. You could feel our room vibrating with the noise.

We tried going downstairs to the television lounge. Well, that was a laugh. There wasn't anywhere to lounge, like a sofa or a comfy armchair. There were just these old vinyl straight-back chairs, the same sort as in the breakfast room, but even older, so you had to play musical chairs finding the ones without the wobbly legs. There wasn't much of a television either. It was supposed to be colour but the switch wouldn't stay stable, so people's faces were gloomy grey for a bit and then suddenly blushed bright scarlet for no reason. There was something wrong with the sound too. It was all blurry and every time anyone talked there was a buzzing sound.

'I'm starting to feel that way myself,' said Mum, putting her hands over her ears.

'Don't throw another moody on me, for goodness sake,' said Mack. 'I can't stick this. I'm going out.'

Mum hunched up even smaller in her chair after he'd gone. I went over to her and tried putting my arm round her. She didn't seem to notice.

'Good riddance to bad rubbish,' I said fiercely.

We both knew where he'd gone. Down the pub. He'd drink all our money and then try to scrounge from some mates. And then he'd come staggering back and be all stupid and snore all night and in the morning he'd have such a sore head he'd snap at the least thing.

I got ten out of ten for an accurate prediction. But by the afternoon he was acting sorry. He'd won a bet down at the betting shop so he took Mum out in the evening while I babysat and then on Sunday morning he got up ever so early. I heard him go out before anyone else was awake. I couldn't help hoping he was maybe doing a runner. But he came back at ten o'clock, staggering again, but this time it was because he was carrying a television.

'I got it for a fiver at a car-boot sale,' he said triumphantly. 'There! Now we don't have to sit in that stupid lounge. We can watch our own telly. Great, eh?'

It wasn't a colour television, just a little old black-and-white portable set. It took ages to retune it when you changed channels, and of course you couldn't get Sky. But it *was* our own television. We could put the sound up so loud you could hardly hear the arguments in 607 and if we tuned into the same programme as the people in 609 it was like we were listening in stereo.

Mum didn't get so droopy now she had the television to watch. She switched on as soon as she woke up and it was still on long after I settled down to sleep. I liked to listen to it as I snuggled under the covers. But sometimes I put my head right down under my duvet and put my hands hard over my ears so that they made their own odd roaring noise and then I switched on this tiny private little television inside my own head. It was much better than the real thing because I could make up all my own programmes.

I was the lady on breakfast television interviewing people in my bedroom

and I was in all the soaps

and I won all the quizzes

and *Gladiators*

and I was in *Blue Peter*

and I was in
lots of films

and best of all I had my very own comedy show
and it was a huge success.

One Slurpy Square of Yorkie Bar

Just when I'd got into this happy little routine at the Royal, Mum went and mucked it all up. She stopped drooping. She started dashing about. She said we weren't going to be stuck in this crummy bed-and-breakfast dump a day longer. She went to the housing department and the social services and the DSS. She armed herself with Hank and Pippa and me, and whenever we were stuck too long in a queue she sent Pippa and me off sniping into enemy territory in quest of a toilet and she primed her Hank hand grenade and set him off howling.

Mum went into battle day after day, but it didn't make any difference to where we lived. We had to stay put because there wasn't anywhere else for us to go. But someone down the Social told Mum about this drop-in centre where the kids could play and you got cheap food, so Mum thought she'd give it a go.

I didn't like the sound of it.

It wasn't that bad actually, just this big room, half of it for the mums and half a crèche for the kids. It was a bit of a crush in the crèche and there was just this one woman going crackers trying to keep all the kids chirpy.

106

We soon got them sorted out.

But then someone from the Council came and said the centre had to be closed because there wasn't any more money to fund it. Mum started moaning and creating, saying this drop-in centre was practically saving her life because we were stuck in a bed-and-breakfast hotel and it was no place for little kids. The Council Someone got a bit stammery because Mum can get ever so fierce when she feels like it, and he promised to put Hank's name down on the day nursery waiting list.

'Oh, very funny,' said Mum. 'He'll be twenty-one before he gets a blooming place.'

'This little girly here will be old enough for proper school soon,' he said, timidly patting Pippa.

Then he turned to me.

Oh-oh. I should have seen it coming and scarpered.

'Why isn't this girl in school, hmm? Now, I *can* help you here. We'll get her registered at the local school straightaway and she can start on Monday morning.'

Thanks a lot.

It had been the one ultra big bonus of life at the Oyal Htl. NO SCHOOL.

I knew Naomi and Funny-Face and most of the other kids at the hotel had to go. I'd hoped I'd not got noticed. I don't like school. Well, my first school was OK. There was a smiley teacher and we could play with pink dough and we all got to sing these soppy old nursery rhymes. I could sing loudest and longest.

But then we moved up to Scotland and I had to go to a new school and it was all different and I got teased because of the way I talk. Then we moved back down South and lived in the flats and that school was the sort where even the little kids get their heads held down the toilet. That was a pretty grim way of getting your hair washed. I didn't go a bundle on that school. But then the next one, my last school, wasn't so bad. That was when we were living in the lovely house and we were almost an ordinary family and even Mack didn't smack. Well, not so much.

It was a bit depressing though. They gave me all these tests and stuff and I couldn't do a lot of it. They thought I was thick. *I* thought I was thick. I had to go to these extra classes to help me with my reading and my writing and my sums. The other kids laughed at me.

I like it when people laugh at my jokes. But I can't stand it when they laugh at *me*.

But I had this really great remedial teacher, Mr Jamieson, only everyone called him Jamie, even us kids. He was very gentle and he didn't yell at you when you couldn't do something. He worked with me and whenever I learnt the least little thing he smiled and stuck his thumb up and said I was doing really fine. So I

felt fine and I learnt a lot more and then Jamie
got me to do some other tests and it turned out
I wasn't thick at all. I was INTELLIGENT.

Jamie asked me about all the other schools
and he said that it was no wonder I hadn't been
able to learn much, because I'd had so many
changes. But now I could get stuck in and
swoop through all the stuff I didn't know and
Jamie said I'd soon end up top of the class, not
bottom. So there.

But then Mack lost his job and we lost our
house and we ended up in the Oyal Htl, miles
and miles and miles away from my old school.

Still, if I had to go to school, that was the one
I wanted to go to. So that I could still see
Jamie.

'Of course you can't go, Elsa. You'd have to
get two buses. And then walk miles. We can't
afford the fares. And you'd wear out your
trainers in weeks. No, you're to go to this
Mayberry School where the other kids go.'

Only they didn't all go, of course. Naomi
went. The Asian kids went. One or two others.
But Funny-Face and nearly all the boys
bunked off every day.

I decided that's what I'd do. I might know I
was intelligent, but this school might give me
the wrong sort of tests. I could easily end up
being thought thick all over again. There was

110

no guarantee at all I'd find another Jamie.

I started hanging around more with Funny-Face and the others. I had to work hard to get them to like me. I had to tell them lots and lots of jokes. They soon got sick of my usual repertoire. Get that fancy word. I'm *not* thick. I know lots and lots of things, though they're not usually the sort of things they like you to know in school. All comedians have to have a repertoire – it's all the jokes in their act. So to impress Funny-Face and his Famous Five followers I had to tell a few rude jokes. Naughty jokes. Blue jokes. Dirty jokes. You know the sort.

The trouble was that Pippa still hung round me most of the time, and she heard some of the jokes too. I told her and told her and told her that she mustn't repeat them, but one time she forgot. She told Mack.

And then guess what. SMACK.

'It wasn't my fault this time,' said Funny-Face afterwards.

'It was my fault,' said Pippa, and she burst into tears.

'You didn't mean to,' I said, giving her a cuddle. 'Here, don't cry, you soppy little thing. It's me he smacked, not you.'

'You don't hardly ever cry,' said Pippa.

'She's tough,' said Funny-Face, and he sounded admiring.

'Yeah, that's me. Tough as old boots,' I said, swaggering.

So on the Monday I was due to start school I set off with Naomi, but the minute we got down the road I veered off with Funny-Face and the Famous Five.

112

'Hey, Elsa. Why don't you come with me?' Naomi said, looking disappointed. 'I thought we were friends. Why do you want to go off with all the boys?'

'We are friends, Naomi. Course we are. I just don't want to go to this dopey old school, that's all. I'll see you after, same as usual, and we'll play in the toilets and have fun.'

'But it isn't a dopey school, really. And I hoped we'd get to be in the same class. I even swopped desks with this other girl so there'd be a place for you to sit beside me.'

'Oh Naomi,' I said, fidgeting. She was starting to make me feel bad. But I really didn't want to go to school. I didn't even want to be in Naomi's class and sit beside her. Naomi looked like she was really brainy, being a bookworm and all that. I knew I was intelligent, Jamie said so, but I hadn't quite caught up with all the things I'd missed, and maybe it would still look as if I was thick. I didn't want Naomi knowing.

So I went off with Funny-Face and the others. I bunked off with them all day long. It was OK for a while. We couldn't hang about the hotel or risk going round the town because someone would spot us and twig we were bunking off school, but we went to this camp place they'd made on a demolition site. It wasn't much of a camp, just some corrugated iron shoved together with a blue tarpaulin for a roof. It was pretty crowded when we were all crammed in there knee-to-knee, and there was nothing to sit on, just cold rubbly ground.

'Well, you could make it a bit comfier, couldn't you?' said Funny-Face.

'Yeah, you fix it up for us, Elsa,' said one of his henchboys.

'Why me?' I said indignantly.

'You're a girl, aren't you?'

I snorted. I wasn't going along with that sort of sexist rubbish. They seemed to think they were Peter Pan and the Lost Boys and I was wet little Wendy.

'Catch me doing all your donkey work,' I said. 'Hey, what do you get if you cross a zebra and a donkey? A zeedonk. And what do you get if you cross a pig and a zebra? Striped sausages.' I kept firing jokes at them as the resident entertainer, and so they stopped expecting me to be the chief cook and bottle-washer into the bargain.

They started bullying the littlest boy, a runny-nosed kid not much older than Pippa, getting him to run round the site finding sacks and stuff for us to sit on. He tripped over a brick and cut both his knees and got more runny-nosed than ever, so I mopped him up and told him a few more jokes to make him laugh. It was heavy going. His name was Simon and he certainly seemed a bit simple. But he was a game little kid and so I stuck up for him when the boys were bossing him around and when we were all squatting on our makeshift cushions and Funny-Face started passing round a crumpled packet of fags, I wouldn't let Simon sample a smoke.

'You don't want to mess around with ciggies, my lad, they'll stunt your growth,' I said firmly, and I gave him a toffee chew instead.

I spurned Funny-Face's fags too. I can't stick the smell and they make me go dizzy and I've seen my mum cough-cough-coughing every morning. But even though Simon and I didn't participate in the smoking session it still got so fuggy in the camp my head started reeling. It came as a relief when the blue tarpaulin suddenly got ripped right off and we were exposed by this other dopey gang of boys also bunking off from school. They threw a whole pile of dust and dirt all over us as we sat there gasping, and then ran away screeching with laughter.

So then, of course, Funny-Face and the Famous Five started breathing fire instead of inhaling it, and they went rampaging across the demolition site to wreak their revenge. I rampaged a bit too, but it all seemed a bit ridiculous to me. There was a pathetic sort of war with both gangs throwing stones rather wildly. Simon got over-excited and wouldn't keep down out of range, so he got hit on the head.

It was only a little bump and graze but it frightened him and he started yelling. The boys just stood about jeering at him, though they looked a bit shamefaced. So I rushed over to him going 'Mee-Maa Mee-Maa Mee-Maa' like an ambulance, and then I made a big production of examining him and pretending his whole head had been knocked off and he needed a major operation. Simon was so simple he believed me at first and started crying harder, but when he twigged it was all a joke he started to enjoy being the centre of attention as a major casualty of war.

The war seemed to have petered out anyway, and the rival gang wandered off down the chip shop because it was nearly lunchtime.

That proved to be a major drawback to bunking off. None of us lot had any lunch. We didn't have any spare cash either. As DSS kids we were entitled to a free school lunch but they just issued you with a ticket, not actual dosh you could spend. So as we weren't at school we were stuck. I began to wish I hadn't been so generous with my toffee chew.

One of the boys found half a Yorkie bar he'd forgotten about right at the bottom of his bomber-jacket pocket. The wrapping paper had disintegrated and the chocolate was liberally sprinkled with little fluffy bits and after he'd passed it round for everyone to nibble it was all slurpy with boy-lick too – but it was food, after all, so I ate a square.

I was still starving all afternoon and getting ever so bored with bunking off. I had to keep an eye on the time so as I knew when to go back to the Oyal Htl as if I'd just been let out of afternoon school. When you keep on looking at the time it doesn't half go s-l-o-w-l-y. Half a century seemed to plod past but it was only half an hour.

But e-v-e-n-t-u-a-l-l-y it was time to be making tracks. And then I found out I'd been wasting my time after all. Mum had decided to trot down to the school with Hank and Pippa to see how I'd got on for my first day. Only I wasn't there, obviously, so she went into the school to find me and of course the teacher said I hadn't ever arrived.

Mum was MAAAAAAAAAD.

And then Mack got in on the act and you can guess what he did.

So I stormed off in a huff all by myself.

I sat there and it hurt where Mack had hit me and my tummy rumbled and I felt seriously fed up. But I didn't cry.

And then I heard footsteps. The clacky-stomp of high heels. It was Mum come to find me. I thought at first she might still be mad, but she sat right down beside me, even though she nearly split her leggings, and she put her arms round me. I did cry a bit then.

'I'm sorry, sausage,' she said, nuzzling into my wild lion's mane. 'I know he's too hard on you sometimes.

118

But it's just that you won't do as you're told. And you've got to go to school, Elsa.'

'It's not fair. I don't want to go to that rotten old school where I don't know anyone.'

'You know that nice Naomi. She's your friend! Oh, come on now, Elsa, you're never *shy*. You!' Mum laughed and tweaked my nose.

'The others all bunk off. The boys.'

'I don't care about them. I care about you. My girl. Now listen. You don't want to go to school. *I* don't want you to go to school. I'd much sooner have you round the hotel keeping the kids quiet for me. I've missed you something chronic today.'

'Really?' I said, cheering up considerably.

'Yes, but *listen*. You've *got* to go to school because it's the law, see, and if you don't go they can say I'm not looking after you properly. You know the Social are always on to us as it is. We don't want to give them any excuse whatsoever to whip you into Care.'

She'd got me there. So I had to go the next morning. I set off with all the other kids – and then when we got to the end of the road, Funny-Face and the Famous Five all called to me.

'Come on then, Elsa.'

'Come with us, eh?'

'Come to the camp.'

Little Simon even came and held my hand and asked if I'd come and play ambulances with him. His face fell a mile when I had to say no. So I gave him a packet of Polos and showed him how to poke his pointy little tongue through the hole. That cheered him up no end.

'Elsa! Why aren't you coming?' said Funny-Face. 'You chicken or something?'

'Hey, why did the one-eyed chicken cross the road? To get to the Bird's Eye shop.'

'That is a fowl joke,' said Funny-Face.

We both cracked up.

'Come on. You can be good fun . . . for a girl,' said Funny-Face.

'You can be quite perceptive . . . for a boy,' I said, and I waved to him and walked off with Naomi.

'Is he your boyfriend then?' she said.

'Look, *I'm* the one that's meant to make the jokes,' I said. 'Him!'

'He fancies you all the same,' said Naomi. 'You and him will be slinking off to room one hundred and ten soon.'

'Naomi!' I nudged her and she nudged me back and we both fell about giggling.

The Manager and the bunny lady can't let Room 110 because the damp's got so bad all the wallpaper's peeled off and the Health Inspector's been round. But someone nicked a spare key and some of the big kids pair off, boy and girl, and sneak into the empty room together. They don't seem to mind the damp.

But catch me going anywhere with Funny-Face. Least of all Room 110.

Naomi and I had a laugh about it, like I said, but as I got nearer and nearer the school there suddenly didn't seem anything to laugh at.

'Cheer up, Elsa. It's OK, really it is. Look, tell me a school joke.'

I swallowed. My mouth had suddenly gone dry. For once I didn't really feel in a jokey mood. Still, a comedienne has to be funny no matter what she feels like.

'OK, so there's this geography teacher, right, and he's asking all the kids where all these mountains are, and he says to the little thick one, "Where are the Andes?" and the little thick one blinks a bit and then pipes up, "At the end of my armies." '

My own andies were cold and clenched tight. I felt like the little thick one all right.

Pizza and Porky-Pies

I was right to feel edgy. I didn't like this new school at all.

I didn't get to sit next to Naomi in her class. I was put in the special class, which was a bit humiliating for a start. They said it was just for a little while, to see how things worked out. Hmm. Fine if they did work out. But what if they didn't? Where do you go if you're too thick even for the special class? Do they march you right back to the Infants?

I didn't like my teacher in this strange class I got stuck in.

122

I wanted a young man teacher like Jamie. Mrs Fisher was old and probably a woman (though she had a moustache above her upper lip).

She also had a hard voice that could rip right through you, though when I first got shoved in her class she stretched her thin lips in a smile and said in ever such sugary, sweetie tones that she was pleased to meet me, and oh what a pretty name Elsa is, and here was my notebook and have this nice sharp pencil, dearie, and why don't you sit at the front where I can see you and write me a little story about yourself.

She was trying to kid on she was really interested in me, but she couldn't fool me. When she took us all out in the playground to have P.E., she got talking to one of the other teachers. The other teacher saw me barging around doing batty things with a bean bag and asked Mrs Fisher who I was. Mrs Fisher didn't even tell her my name. She just said: 'Oh, that's just one of the bed-and-breakfast children.'

I'm not even a she. I'm a That. Some sort of boring blob who doesn't have a name, who doesn't even have a sex.

Elsa the Blob. Hey, I quite like that idea. I could be a great big giant monster Blob and squelch around obliterating people. Mack is still first on my list but Mrs Fisher comes a close second.

I wrote her a little story about myself all right. I wrote that my real name is Elsarina and I'm a child star – actress, singer and comedienne – and I've been in lots of adverts on the telly and done panto and heaps of musicals, and I was actually currently starring in a travelling repertory performance of *Annie* – me playing Annie, of course. And I wrote that my mum and the rest of my family are all in showbiz too, part of the company, and *that's* why we're currently living in a hotel, because we travel around putting on our shows.

I tried to make it sound dead convincing. But when she read it she just gave me one of those smug old smiles.

'This is certainly some story, dear,' she said. 'Rather a *fairy* story, I'm afraid.'

The other kids tittered, though they didn't know what she was on about. She handed me my story back with all my spelling and punctuation mistakes underlined. There seemed to be more red ink on the page than pencil.

But I was not deterred. If I was meant to be thick then some of the kids in the class were as dense as drains, and gurgled into the bargain. So I tried out my Elsarina story on them, and they were all dead impressed, even the big tough guys. I gave them a few quick samples of my comic routine out in the playground and some of them laughed and then I treated them to a rendition of 'The Sun Will Come Out Tomorrow'. I forget what a powerful voice I've got. One or two of them ran for cover, but those that stayed seriously seemed to appreciate my performance.

School didn't seem quite so bad at this stage. I had my little group of fans who happily drank in everything I told them. I got a bit carried away and started elaborating about my mum being this really beautiful actress and yet she could belt out a song and dance up a storm in this really classy cabaret act . . . and every so often I seemed to step outside myself and hear my own voice and I could see I was tempting fate telling all these lies. Well, they weren't completely lies. Mum *did* use to be beautiful before she met up with Mack and had some more kids so that she lost her lovely figure and gained a few worry lines. She could *still* look beautiful if only she'd bother to slap on some make-up and do her hair properly. She really did use to sing and dance too. She'd sing along to all the records on the radio in a happy husky voice and she'd dance away, wiggling her hips and waggling her fingers. So Mum *could* sing and dance and if only she'd had the right breaks then I'm sure she really could be a star . . .

All the same, I shut up at lunchtime when I met Naomi. It was great to have my own special friend to wander round the playground with. School dinners weren't so bad either. They weren't a patch on my Mega-Feast at home with Pippa, but you were allowed to choose what you wanted, so I had a big plateful of pizza and chips, and I set all our lunch table laughing with a whole load of pizza jokes that aren't fit for publication. Even my silly old chip joke went down well salted.

'Hey, you lot, what are hot, greasy and romantic? Chips that pass in the night!'

The afternoon wasn't so great because we had to divide up into groups to do all this dumb weighing and measuring. I could do that easy-peasy but I didn't have much clue when it came to how you write it all down. I didn't want to admit this so I made a lot of it up, and then of course Mrs Fisher came nosing around and when she saw all my calculations she sighed and scored a line right through them, so it was obvious to everyone I'd got it all wrong. She sat down with me and tried to explain how to do it. I felt stupid in front of all the others and so I couldn't take it in. She had to go through the whole gubbins again, speaking e-v-e-r s-o s-l-o-w-l-y because she obviously thought she had a right moron on her hands. The other kids started to snigger by this stage, so when Mrs Fisher at last left us in peace I had to work hard to regain their respect. I started on about my stage clothes and my mum's stage clothes and my little sister Pip-pa's stage clothes, and once I'd started on Pippa I couldn't stop, and soon I'd turned her into this adorable little child star with chubby cheeks and a head of curls and though she hadn't started school yet she could sing and dance like a real little trooper.

I was certainly going a bit over the top here, because even Mack and Mum admit that Pippa is plain. Well, the poor kid can't help it, being lumbered with Mack as a dad. She hasn't got chubby cheeks, she hasn't got curls (Mum did have a go with her curling tongs once when Pippa was going to a party but her hair ended up looking like it had exploded). She isn't even little – she's nearly as big as me though she's half my age – and as for singing and dancing, well, Pippa can't ever remember the words to any song, let alone the tune, and the only sort of dancing she can do is slam-dancing, though she doesn't *mean* to barge straight into you.

But I built her up into such a little Baby Wonder that the kids in my class were drooling, and they all wanted to see the show with me and this mega-brilliant little brat and our glamorous movie-star mummy.

'Sorry, folks, we've been sold out for weeks because the show's so popular,' I said breezily, though my heart was beating fit to bust.

That shut them up for a few seconds, but then I started to wonder about going-home time. Mum had caught me out yesterday by trailing round to the school. What if she did it again today? What if she'd just pulled on her oldest old T-shirt and leggings and hadn't bothered to do her hair? All the children would see her for themselves. And even if I could somehow manage to convince them that she was just practising for a forthcoming searingly realistic drama on the telly about a careworn young mother ground down by the system, they'd see Pippa too.

It might help matters if my whole family were present and correct. I could tell them that Mack was all set for a remake of King Kong. He didn't even need to bother with a costume.

I shot out of school the moment the bell went. It was a huge great relief to see that Mum wasn't there, though I couldn't help feeling a weeny bit miffed all the same, because she *said* she'd come. She wasn't back at the hotel either. None of them were. I couldn't get into room 608 because I didn't have a key, so I had to mooch about the corridors for ages. Naomi came along but she was a bit narked with me because I hadn't waited for her after school, and she couldn't play with me now anyway because she had to help her mum with her brothers. Then Funny-Face sloped into view, scuffing his trainers and spitting. He was even more narked with me because my mum had stirred things up yesterday and the school had done a check on their registers and sent the truant officer round and now Funny-Face and the Famous Five had to turn up at school tomorrow or *else*.

'Or else you'll all get into trouble and Elsa'll get into trouble for getting you lot into trouble,' I said, pulling a funny face at Funny-Face.

He didn't pull one back. He called me a lot of rude names, even the infamous one he wrote on the wall that I had to correct.

I swept away loftily and pretended I didn't care. But I felt a bit friendless by now. And I was starting to get dead worried that I might be familyless too.

Why had they all pushed off without telling me where they were going? What if they'd finally got fed up with me and packed up and scarpered? I knew Mack didn't want me. He'd go like a shot and he'd take Pippa and Hank because they were his kids and he cared about them. But Mum wouldn't walk out on me, would she? Although only this morning, when the drains all went wrong and someone else's dirty water came bubbling up in our basin, she burst into tears and said she couldn't stick this rotten dump a day longer. So maybe . . . maybe she had gone too.

The ceiling suddenly seemed a long long way off. I felt I was getting smaller and smaller until I wasn't much more than a squeak. I hunched up on the floor with my head on my knees and held on tight in case I disappeared altogether.

'Elsa? What on earth are you doing? What's up, eh?' said Mum, coming down the corridor.

Yes, it was Mum, and I was so very pleased to see her even though she sounded cross. And I was very pleased to see Pippa even though she was all sniffly with her nose running. And I was very pleased to see Hank even though he was howling his head off and needing his nappy changed. And I was ... No. I wasn't very pleased to see Mack. I wouldn't ever go *that* far.

'Where have you *been*? I've been back from school ages and ages!'

'Yeah, well, I'm sorry, love, but it's not our fault. We had a right ding-dong with that useless Manager this morning because we're all going to end up getting typhoid or cholera stuck in this poxy dump, and the tight-fisted pig won't even send for a plumber to fix things, would you believe! Anyway, he said we could clear off if we didn't like it here, and so I said we were doing our best to do just that, but we didn't have any place to go, so *then* we went down the Housing Office, all of us, and would you believe they kept us waiting *all* day. They weren't even going to see us at all because we didn't have some stupid appointment, but we sat it out and I knew you'd be waiting, pet, but I couldn't do anything, could I?'

'So what happened, Mum? Are we getting a house?'

'Are we heck,' said Mum. 'They just mumbled on about priority families and exceptional circumstances and said even if this dump was affecting our health we'd have to get some really bad complaint and it would all have to be written up in medical reports and even then, if we were all at death's door, they couldn't blooming well guarantee us a house or even a mouldy old flat like we used to have.'

'So I asked what *would* guarantee us a house – did one of you kids have to snuff it altogether, is that it?' Mack said. 'It's getting dangerously close too. Look at little Pippa, all sniffles. She can't get rid of that cold, and as for the baby, well, I don't like the sound of his chest at all.'

Mack sighed over Hank, who was still exercising his magnificent lungs. They certainly sounded in full working order.

'Yeah, Mack started to get really stroppy. Well, I did too, especially when they said they couldn't even guarantee us a proper set of rooms here like we're entitled to, instead of us having to squash up like sardines. They said there was nothing further they could do at this moment in time, and threatened to set the police on to us unless we left the office.'

Mum sighed theatrically, the back of her hand to her forehead. She mightn't be a proper actress but it certainly sounded as if she'd been giving a good performance down at the Housing Office. She threatened to go back again tomorrow, wondering if she could get us rehoused by sheer persistence.

'Yes, good thinking, Mum,' I said, encouraging her so she wouldn't come to collect me from school and crack my credibility.

Only I needn't have bothered. Someone else started telling the wrong sort of tales the very next day. Someone with a funny face. And a great big mouth.

Funny-Face got shoved in the special class too. Right next to me, at the front, under the Fisher's pop eyes. This reminded me of 101 Popeye the Sailorman jokes — *you* know — and I swopped some of them with Funny-Face and we both got terrible snorty giggles, and Mrs Fisher's eyes popped so much they almost rolled down her cheeks, and her mouth went so tight her lips disappeared.

'I'm glad you two are finding school so amusing,' she said, dead sarcastic. 'Perhaps you'd like to share your little jokes with me, hmm?'

Perhaps not. If she heard some of the wilder Popeye jokes she'd go off pop herself.

So Funny-Face and I were getting on famously until playtime. And then one of the kids in the class asked if Funny-Face performed too.

'You what?' said Funny-Face.

'Are you a child star like Elsarina and Pipette?' They elaborated on the famous fictional talents of me and my family, and Funny-Face fell about, thinking this was just another joke, a wind-up on my part.

'You lot aren't half loopy,' said Funny-Face. 'How come you've fallen for all this rubbish? Elsa isn't a famous star! She's just a bed-and-breakfast kid, like me. And cripes, you should see her mum and her dopey little sister — stars!'

That was enough. Funny-Face saw stars then. Because I punched him right in the nose.

All the children started shouting 'Fight! Fight! Fight!' I was all set to have a proper fight even though I'm generally gentle, and Funny-Face was bewildered but wanted a fight too because I'd made his nose bleed. But as soon as we'd squared up to each other Mrs Fisher came flying forth and she seized Funny-Face in one hand and me in the other. She shook us both very vigorously indeed, practically clonking our heads together, and told us we were very rough, naughty children and we had to learn not to be violent in school.

Then, as she stalked off, she said just one word. Well, she muttered it, but I heard. And Funny-Face did too. She said, *'Typical.'* She meant we were typical bed-and-breakfast kids indulging in typical disruptive behaviour. And I suddenly felt sick, as if I needed my bed and might well throw up my breakfast.

Funny-Face didn't look too clever either. He wiped the smear of blood from his nose and pulled a hideous face at Mrs Fisher's back, crossing his eyes and waggling his tongue.

I giggled feebly.

'Why did the teacher have crossed eyes, eh? Because she couldn't control her pupils.'

It was one of my least funny jokes but Funny-Face guffawed politely.

'Well, she's not going to control us, is she, Elsa?'

'You bet she's not.' His nose was still bleeding. I felt up my sleeve for a crumpled tissue. 'Here,' I said, dabbing at him.

'Leave off! You're acting like my mum,' said Funny-Face.

'Sorry I socked you one,' I said.

'Yeah, well, if that old trout hadn't come along I'd have flattened you, see. Just as well for you. Though you can hit quite hard – for a girl.'

'If you start that I'll hit you even harder,' I said, but I gave his nose another careful wipe. 'We're still mates, aren't we?'

'Course we are. Though why did you have to attack me like that, eh?'

'Because of what you said about my mum and my sister.'

'But you were the one telling porky-pies, not me! Why did you spin all those stupid stories about them? I mean, it's daft. As if you lot could ever be in showbiz.'

'We could, you know,' I said fiercely. 'Well, maybe not my mum. Or Pippa. But *I'm* going to be some day. I'll be famous, just you wait and see. I'll be a comedienne – that's a lady who tells jokes – and I'll have my own show and I'll get to be on the telly, you'll see, maybe sooner than you think.'

It was sooner than I thought, too. Because when Funny-Face and I went home from school that day there was a camera crew filming in the foyer of the Royal Hotel!

Television
and no
Tea

'What on earth's going on?' said Funny-Face.
'Hey, is this for telly? Are we going to be on the
telly?'

He pulled a grotesque funny face for the
camera, waving both his arms.

I sighed scornfully. I wasn't going to behave
like some idiotic amateur. I eyed up all the
people and spotted the man in the tightest
jeans and the leather jacket. That one just had
to be the director. I walked right up to him,
smiling.

'Hello, I'm Elsa, I live here and I'm going to
be a comedienne when I grow up. In fact, I've
got my whole comedy act worked out right
now. Would you like to listen?'

The director blinked rapidly behind his trendy glasses, but he seemed interested.

'You live here, do you, Elsa? Great, well, we're doing a programme called *Children in Crisis*, OK? Shall we do a little interview with you and your friend, eh? You can tell us all about how awful it is to have to stay in a bed-and-breakfast hotel, right?'

'Wrong, wrong, wrong!' said the bunny lady receptionist, rushing out from behind her desk. Even the telephonist lady had chucked her Jackie Collins and was peering out from behind her glass door, all agog.

'Go and get the Manager, quick,' the bunny lady commanded, shooing the telephonist lady up the corridor. 'Now listen to me, you television people. You're trespassing. Get out of this hotel right this minute or I'll call the police and have you evicted.'

'I can tell any joke you like. We'll have a police joke, OK? What did the policeman say to the three-headed man? Hello hello hello. Where does the policeman live? Nine nine nine Let's be Avenue. What's the police dog's telephone number? Canine canine canine.'

'Very funny, dear,' said the director, though he didn't laugh. 'Now, once we get the camera rolling I want you to say a bit about the crowded room you live in and how damp it is and maybe there are nasty bugs in the bath, yeah?'

'How dare you! This is a scrupulously clean establishment, there are no bugs here, no infestations of any kind!' the bunny lady screeched, so cross that the fluff on her jumper quivered.

'Bugs, OK, I'll tell you an insect joke, right? You've got this fly and this flea, yes, and when they fly past each other what time is it? Fly past flea.' I laughed to show that this was the punchline.

'Mmm, well. Simmer down now, sweetie, we

want you looking really sad for the camera. And you, sonnie, do you think you could stop pulling those faces for five seconds?'

'OK, I can look sad, it's all part of a comedienne's repertoire. Look, is this sad enough?'

'Well, you needn't go to extremes. Cheer up just a bit.'

'Hey, I've thought of another insect joke. There were these two little flies running like mad over a cornflake packet – and do you know why? Because it said, "Tear along dotted line".'

I laughed, but that made me cheer up a bit too much. And then the Manager came charging up and started shouting and swearing at the television people and they tried to film him and he put his hand over the camera and I started to get the feeling I might have lost my big chance to make it on to the television.

'Phone the police this minute!' the Manager commanded.

'I know some more police jokes,' I said, but no-one was listening.

'Who put you up to this? Who invited you in, eh? Has one of the residents been complaining? Which one? You tell me. If they don't like it here they can get out,' the Manager shouted, making wild gestures. He nearly clipped me on the head and I ducked. 'It was your mum and dad, wasn't it, little girl!'

'That man's not my dad.'

'The big Scottish bloke, he was throwing his weight around and moaning about his basin.'

'What animal do you find in a toilet? A wash-hand bison,' I said, but I seemed to have lost my audience.

The police arrived and there was a big argy-bargy which ended in the camera crew having to squeeze all their stuff back round the revolving door, while the Manager continued to rant and rave to me, saying it was all my family's fault and we'd better start packing our bags right this minute.

I began to feel very much like a Child in Crisis. I whizzed out after the camera crew, desperate for one last chance to get on the telly.

'Hey, don't go, don't pack up!' I yelled, as I saw them heaving their gear into a van. 'Look, couldn't we do an interview in front of the hotel, eh? I'll be ever so sad – I could even try to cry if you like. Look, I can make my face crumple up – or I tell you what, I'll go and get my little sister and brother from our room, they're great at crying—'

'Sorry, sweetie, but I think this is a waste of time,' said the director. 'I don't need this sort of hassle. And besides, you're a great little sport but you're not the sort of kid I'm looking for. I need someone . . . ' He waved his hand in the air, unable to express exactly what he wanted. Then he stopped and stood still.

'Someone like that little kid there!' he said, snapping his fingers.

I looked for this favoured little kid. And do you know who it was? Naomi, mooching along the road, trailing a brother in either hand, looking all fed up and forlorn because I'd rushed off with Funny-Face instead of waiting for her.

'Hey, sweetie, over here!' The director waved at her frantically. 'Where did you spring from, hmm? You don't live in the bed-and-breakfast hotel by any chance?'

Naomi nodded nervously, clutching her little brothers tight.

'Great!' He threw back his head and addressed the clouds. 'A gift!'

'We don't want any gifts. We don't take stuff from strangers,' said Naomi, and she started trying to hustle her brothers away. She hustled a little too abruptly, and Neil tripped and started crying.

'Hey, shut up, little squirt,' said Funny-Face. 'You're going to be on the telly. Can I still be on it too, mister?'

'And me?' I said urgently.

'Well, you can maybe sort of wander in the background,' said the director. 'But no clowning. No funny faces. And absolutely *no* jokes.'

I didn't actually feel like cracking any jokes right that minute. Naomi was going to be the star of the show. Not me, even though I'd been perfecting my routine and practising on everyone all this time. Naomi, who couldn't crack a joke to save her life, little meek and mousey Naomi!

OK, I thought. Maybe just *one* joke to try to cheer myself up. So I whispered all to myself,

'What do you get if you cross an elephant with a mouse? Socking great holes in the skirting board!' I couldn't help laughing. You can't really do that quietly. The director glared in my direction. 'Dear goodness, you dippy kids! I don't want merriment, I don't want laughter, I don't want JOKES.'

'OK, OK, no jokes,' I said, and I pinched my lips together with my fingers so he could see I was serious. Only it was such a pity. The mouse and elephant joke had triggered off a whole herd of elephant jokes inside my head, and they were trumpeting tremendously.

What do elephants do in the back of a Mini? Play squash.

What's grey and wrinkled and lights up? An electric elephant.

What's big and red and hides its face in the corner? An embarrassed elephant.

'Well *I* can't tell jokes,' said Naomi truthfully. 'I can't dance or sing or anything. So you'd really better pick Elsa.'

'Oh Naomi,' I said, immensely touched. 'You can't do all the showy things, but you're ever so brainy. You could get to be on one of the quiz shows, eh?'

'Never mind quiz shows. This little girl's perfect for *Children in Crisis*. Now just stand here, sweetie – little brothers too, that's it, and I'll ask you a few questions while the camera rolls, right?'

'No, wait! Neil, come and get your nose wiped and stop that silly sniffling,' Naomi said urgently. 'And you, Nicky, pull your socks up.'

'No, we want you just as you are, runny nose and all! Now, I want you to tell me how miserable it is in the hotel and how your little brothers keep crying and how lousy it is not to have enough money for lots of dolls and video games like other kids. OK, action!'

Naomi chewed her lip anxiously, not going into action at all. She was thinking hard.

'It *is* miserable sometimes. But my mum gives me a cuddle or I read my book or my friend Elsa tells me a joke and then I cheer up.'

I cheered up too, but the director seemed determined to damp everything down. He practically told Naomi what she had to say.

The first time she had a go she came out all weird and wooden, and she kept looking up at the director anxiously and hissing, 'Is that right? Have I remembered it?'

'No, sweetie, don't keep saying that. Just act natural, for pity's sake,' said the director, practically tearing his hair.

The bunny lady receptionist came clopping out into the street in her high heels, wagging her pointed nails at the television crew.

'Now look! You're harassing our tenants. We'll call the police again. The Manager's on the phone right this minute. And as for you kids, I'm warning you. We don't have to house you, you know. If you've got any complaints then you can push off somewhere else.'

She clip-clopped back into the hotel. Naomi stared after her worriedly, her eyes filling with tears.

'Does she mean that? She wouldn't really throw us out, would she?' Naomi whispered. 'We haven't got anywhere else to go. And it's so unfair, because we've put up with ever such

149

a lot – we've even had those horrible bugs, cockroaches, squiggling all over the floor. One even got in the toe of our baby Nathan's bootee, and yet the Manager wouldn't even send for the pest-control people. He said it was our fault because we were dirty! And my mum cried when he said that because we're as clean as we can be – we bath every day even when there isn't any hot water, and my mum keeps the room spotless, and that's not easy with the four of us kids. I don't know what we're going to do, because we've been waiting six months and we still can't get a flat and if we get turned out the hotel then us kids will have to go into Care and we've got to stay with our mum.'

'We want our mum,' said Nicky.

'Mum! Mum!' wailed Neil.

'Perfect!' said the director. The cameras had been rolling for all of Naomi's outburst. 'Absolutely great, sweetie. Lovely emotive stuff. Right folks, I think we can hit the road now.'

'But what about us?' said Naomi, wiping her eyes. 'Are we going to get thrown out?'

'Mmm? Oh, I shouldn't think so,' he said vaguely.

He'd turned his back on us. He didn't know. He didn't even care. He just wanted to make a good television programme.

I put my arm round Naomi.
'We'll be OK,' I said, giving her a hug. 'Don't take any notice of him. He's just been using us. Still, it looks like you really will be on the telly after all, Naomi.'

Naomi didn't seem very thrilled about the idea. She still worried and worried that her family might get thrown out.

'Look, they've threatened us too. That Manager thinks it's all my mum and Mack's fault. We'll all be thrown out together. We'll have to set up a little camp. It's OK, Naomi. Don't get in such a state.'

I tried to cheer her up, but it wasn't easy.

'I wish you hadn't got us all involved with those telly people,' Naomi said, sighing.

That's what Mum and Mack were saying too in room 608. Only they were saying it a lot more angrily. I could hear them yelling from right down the corridor.

'Oh-oh,' I said.

'It's all your fault, you stupid Scottish git!' Mum was screaming. 'You shouldn't have phoned them. Now that Manager will make our lives a misery.'

'It's a flaming misery as it is. It couldn't be worse. I was simply trying to help, so stop giving me all this hassle, woman.'

I slunk into the room. Pippa was crouched in the duck cot, clutching Baby Pillow. Hank was grizzling in bed, needing his nappy changed. I mopped them up and crept off with them. I don't think Mum and Mack even noticed.

It was getting near teatime and there were lots of cooking smells coming from the kitchen. Mum still said it was a filthy hole and we couldn't cook in there or we'd go down with a terrible disease. I was starting to get so starving hungry I was willing to risk the terrible disease, but we didn't have anything to cook.

Naomi's mum was stirring a very interesting bean stew that smelt ever so rich and tasty. She had baby Nathan on her hip, and he was smacking his lips in happy anticipation.

Naomi told her mum all about the television people and the Manager's threats, but Naomi's mum didn't get mad at all. She just went on stirring her stew.

'We'll be fine, little old lady,' she said to Naomi. 'You're such a worry-guts. Here, tea's just about ready. Have you got the plates set out in our room?'

She saw Pippa and Hank and me looking at her hungrily.

'Do you kids want to come and join us for tea?' she said cheerily.

We wanted to extremely badly, but there didn't look that much of a stew and it seemed a bit mean to eat their food so I said we'd be having our own tea in a minute.

But when I did a quick sortie back to room 608 the row was getting louder and fiercer and I knew there was no point disturbing them. So Pippa and Hank and I hung around the kitchen some more. Simple Simon's mum came along and she cooked a whole load of chips in the greasy old chip-pan – so many that they almost came bubbling over the top. They smelt so good and she had such a lot that I decided we'd have a few if we got offered. Only we didn't.

Simon's mum is very fierce.

'What are you kids staring at?' she said

sharply. 'Clear off out of it. Go and get your own tea.'

But that was easier said than done. The row was still roaring. So we sat outside the room, our tummys rumbling. Mack came storming out eventually. He tripped right over me actually. I felt like calling him a Great Scottish Git too, but I sensed it wasn't quite the moment. I knew where he was going. Down the pub. And he wouldn't be back for ages.

At least that meant we could get in our room. But Mum didn't seem up to considering something ordinary like tea. She was in bed crying and when I tried to talk to her she pulled the covers up over her head. She went on crying for a bit and then she went to sleep.

I felt really funny for about five minutes. Not funny ha-ha. Funny peculiar and horrible. It hadn't been a good day. I wasn't going to be on television. I didn't have any tea. I felt like getting into my own bed and pulling the covers up and having a good cry.

But Pippa and Hank were looking up at me and I couldn't let them down. I switched on the telly and said they could stay up as long as they liked because Mum was asleep and Mack was out. And I hunted round the room for food and found some stale sliced bread and a pot of raspberry jam.

'We're going to have a really special tea, you'll see,' I said, scrabbling through Mum's handbag for her nail scissors. I got snipping and scraping and made us ultra-special jam sandwiches.

I made a clown jam sandwich for Hank.

I made a teddy jam sandwich for Pippa and Baby Pillow.

And I made a great red movie-star-lip jam sandwich for me,

and the jammy lips kissed me for being such a good girl.

I woke up early and read my joke books in bed . . .

Why are tall people lazier than short people? Because they're longer in bed, ha ha!

. . . and then Pippa woke up for a cuddle and Hank woke up for a bottle and soon it was time to get up.

Mum didn't wake up. Mack didn't wake up either. He was snoring like a warthog with catarrh.

So I had to speak up to make myself heard.

Mum stirred at last.

'Will you stop that shouting, Elsa!'

'I'm *not* shouting,' I said, wounded. 'I'm simply speaking up a little because that Scottish git is snoring fit to bust.'

Mum stirred more vigorously.

'Don't you dare call Mack names like that, you cheeky little whatsit!'

'But that's what *you* called him just last night.'

We started to have a little argument. I might have got a bit heated. Suddenly the warthog stopped snoring. It reared up in the bed, a horrible sight.

'If you don't stop that shouting and screaming right this minute, Elsa, I'll give you such a smacking you'll never dare say another word.'

He glared at me with his bleary eyes and then slowly subsided back under the covers. Hank gave a worried hiccup. Pippa started sucking her fingers. I blinked hard at the bulk in the bed. I opened my mouth, but Pippa shook her head and clutched me with her dribbly little hands. I gave her a hug to show her it was OK. I wasn't going to speak. Mack might be an idle lout but he doesn't make idle threats. He always follows them through.

I waggled my tongue very impressively at

the bed instead. Mum still had her eyes open but she didn't tell me off. When I went to take Pippa and Hank downstairs for breakfast she sat up in bed and held her arms out to me.

'I'm sorry, love,' she whispered. 'I didn't mean to get you into trouble. You're a good girl really, I know you are. I don't know what I'd do without you.'

I cheered up a bit then, but when we went down to breakfast the bunny lady said loudly to the switchboard lady: 'Oh-oh, there's one of the little trouble-makers.' She pointed at me

with a lilac fingernail to match a new purple fluffy jumper. 'The Manager wants to see your dad in his office,' she announced.

'He's not my dad,' I said and walked straight past, Hank on my hip, Pippa hanging on my hand.

'Mack is my dad,' Pippa whispered. 'Is he going to get into trouble, Elsa?'

'I don't know,' I said uncomfortably. Maybe we were all in trouble. Maybe we really were going to get chucked out.

We went to sit with Naomi and her family at breakfast. They were looking dead gloomy too. Naomi's mum didn't smile at me the way she usually did.

'I'll tell you a really good joke about cornflakes,' I said.

'No jokes, Elsa,' she said, sighing.

'OK, I'll tell you this cornflake joke tomorrow. It's a cereal,' I said. I roared with laughter. It wasn't *that* funny, but I wanted to lighten the atmosphere.

Naomi's mum stayed resolutely gloomy. Naomi chewed her lip anxiously. Even Nicky and Neil couldn't crack a smile.

'What's up, eh?' I said, starting to feed baby Nathan, playing the aeroplane game.

He at least seemed happy enough to play, but Naomi's mum caught hold of my arm and took away my spoon.

'No, leave him be. Leave all my family be. Haven't you done enough?'

'Oh, Mum,' said Naomi. 'It isn't Elsa's fault.'

'She was the one who talked you into that television interview,' said Naomi's mum. 'And now the Manager says we'll have to go.'

'Well, he says we've got to go too. But he doesn't mean it. He just wants to scare us,' I said. I tried to sound reassuring but I was getting scared too. 'Look, I'll go and see the Manager. I'll tell him it was all down to me if you like. Then at least you'll be OK.'

So after we'd had breakfast I lumped Hank along to the Manager's office, Pippa trailing behind us. I didn't have a hand free to knock so we just went barging straight into his office. The Manager wasn't on his own. He wasn't having a little cuddle with the bunny lady. He was with Mrs Hoover, and he didn't look at all cuddly. He was telling Mrs Hoover off, wagging his finger at her.

'What's the matter?' I said. 'Why is he being nasty to you, Mrs Hoover?'

'You! Out of my office this instant,' said the Manager. 'It's your mum and dad I want to see, not you lot.'

'I keep telling you, I haven't *got* a dad. That Scottish bloke is nothing to do with me,' I insisted.

'Oh yes! Thank you for reminding me. Yes, my receptionist informs me that there's more disgusting graffiti about a Scots person inside the ladies' downstairs cloakroom,' said the Manager, still wag-wag-wagging that finger at poor Mrs Hoover.

'She didn't do that! I know for a fact that Mrs Hoover didn't write all that stuff on the walls,' I said quickly, my heart thumping. Everyone seemed to be getting into trouble because of me and it was awful. I decided to make a clean breast of things. (What a weird expression. I haven't got a breast yet for a start. And it wasn't even clean because the basin in room 608 was getting so gungy I hadn't felt very much like washing recently.)

'All the Mack jokes – they're mine,' I said.

The Manager and Mrs Hoover both blinked at me.

'You wrote all that revolting rubbish?' said the Manager.

'I thought some of the jokes were quite funny,' I mumbled.

'You children! Vandals! Hooligans!' said the Manager.

'It was just me. Not Pippa. She can't write yet – and even if she could, she quite likes her dad. It's just me that can't stick him. But you can stop telling Mrs Hoover off because, like I said, it was me.'

'Oh Elsa,' said Mrs Hoover. 'He knows I didn't write it, silly. He's cross because I can't clean it all off. Only I keep telling him, that felt-tip just won't budge even though I scrub and scrub.'

162

'I never see you scrubbing. The hotel is a disgrace. No wonder we have television crews traipsing in here making trouble. If I'm reported to the authorities it will be all your fault.'

'If you get reported to the authorities it'll be because you run a lousy hotel,' said Mrs Hoover. 'How can I possibly hope to keep a huge place like this anywhere near up to standard? Why don't you employ more staff?'

'I'll be employing one less member of staff if you don't watch your tongue,' said the Manager.

'All right then. That suits me. You can stick your stupid job,' said Mrs Hoover, whipping off her overall and throwing it right in his face.

Then she turned on her heel and flounced straight out of his office. I decided it wasn't quite the right time to plead Naomi's case to the Manager. I ran after Mrs Hoover instead.

'Oh gosh, have you really lost your job now? And it's my fault because I did all the scribbling on the walls,' I wailed. 'Oh Mrs Hoover, I'm so sorry!'

'Mrs Whoosit?' said Mrs Hoover. 'Here, is that what you kids call me? Well, don't you fret yourself, pet. I've had it up to here hoovering for that dreadful man. I'll get another cleaning job, they're not that hard to come by even nowadays.'

But I couldn't be absolutely sure she was telling the truth. I wished I was as little as Pippa so she could pick me up and give me a big hug to reassure me. I felt little inside. And stupid. And sad. And sorry.

I was extra loud and noisy and bouncy and bossy at school to try to make myself feel big again. It didn't work. I kept telling jokes to Funny-Face and he kept laughing, but Mrs Fisher was frowning and she made us stay in at playtime and write out I MUST LEARN TO BEHAVE PROPERLY IN THE CLASSROOM fifty times.

Funny-Face is not very good at writing. His words wobble up over the line and slide down below it. His spelling's a bit wobbly too. He missed out one of the 's's in classroom. Mrs Fisher pointed this out huffily. I was scared she might make him do it all over again, so I tried to lighten things a little.

'Why can't you remember there are two 's's in class?' she said crossly. 'I've told you enough times.'

'Which 's' did he leave out this time, Mrs Fisher?' I said.

It was a joke. A bit of a feeble one, but a joke all the same. Only Mrs Fisher just thought I was being cheeky.

Do you know what happened? We had to stay in at lunchtime too. Funny-Face had to write out CLASSROOM another fifty times, and I had to write out a fresh fifty: I MUST LEARN NOT TO BE CHEEKY IN THE CLASSROOM.

'That's silly, anyway,' I muttered. 'That sounds like I can be cheeky in the hall and cheeky in the corridors and cheeky in the toilets and cheeky all over the place. And I wasn't blooming cheeky to start with. I was just joking.'

'You and your
@!+!@ jokes!'
said Funny-Face,
laboriously drawing 's's.

'Hey, don't be like that. Listen, this boy was kept in at lunchtime just like us and his teacher said he had to write out this sentence of not less than fifty words, right? So do you know what he wrote?'

'No, and I don't care,' said Funny-Face. 'Here, I've got all these poxy 's's in the right place, haven't I?'

'Yes. Though hang on, you've started to miss out your 'o's now. There are two in classroom. Like us two in this classroom. But listen to the punchline bit of my joke. This boy wrote, "I went to call my cat in for the night so I stood at the door and called: 'Here, kitty, kitty, kitty, kitty, kitty . . . ' " '

'Shut *up*, Elsa.'

'No, I haven't done enough kittys – there are supposed to be fifty. And you've missed out another 'o' there – *and* there.'

'You'll be going O in a minute, when I punch you right in the nose,' Funny-Face growled.

'What do you give a pig with a sore nose? Oinkment,' I said, snorting like a little pig myself because I think that's one of my funnier jokes.

Funny-Face didn't think it funny at all.

'Why don't you shut your cakehole?' he said, and he sounded so menacing I did what he said.

I wished he hadn't used that expression. We still hadn't been allowed to have our dinners and I kept thinking very wistfully of cake. When horrible old Mrs Fisher eventually let us go, we had to squeeze in right at the end of second-sitting dinners, when all the goodies had long since gone. Not one chip left. We had to make do with a salad, and no-one ever chooses bunny food from choice. I know some excellent bunny jokes but I decided it might be better to keep them in their burrow in my head. Funny-Face still didn't look ready for mirth as he chomped his way morosely through his lettuce.

We had a new teacher in the hall in the afternoon to take us for singing. It was a relief to be free of the Fishy-Eye and I was all set to sing my cares away. I didn't know many of the songs but I've always been good at improvising. So I threw back my head and let rip. But

the teacher stopped playing the piano. Her
face was all screwed up as if she had a terrible
headache.

'Who is making that . . . noise?' she asked.

We stared at her. What did she mean? We
were all making a noise. We were singing.

Only she didn't seem to appreciate that. She
made us start again, this time without the
piano. I decided not to let this faze me. I sang
out joyfully. The teacher shuddered.

'You!' she said, pointing.

I peered round. No, it wasn't anyone else.
She was pointing at me.

'Yes, you. The little bed-and-breakfast girl.'

The other children around me sniggered. I

felt my face start to burn, like the Royal Hotel's toast.

'Could you try not to sing so loudly, please?' said the teacher.

'Why?' I said, astonished.

'Because you're singing rather flat, dear. And completely out of tune. In fact, it might be better if you didn't sing at all, even softly. How about just nodding your head in time to the music?'

The other kids collapsed, nudging each other and tittering.

'Some stage star, eh! She can't even sing in tune,' they hissed.

I had to spend the whole singing lesson with my mouth shut, nid-nodding away like Little Noddy. I didn't feel much like making a noise after that. I hardly said anything on the way home from school. Funny-Face kept having a go at me, but I didn't respond.

'What's up, Elsa?' said Naomi, putting her arm round me. 'Here, I'm sorry my mum got mad at you. It wasn't really fair for her to pick on you.'

'Oh, I don't know. That's what everyone does. Pick on me,' I said gloomily.

'Hey, don't be like that. You're always so cheerful. I can't bear it when you're all sad. Tell us a joke, go on.'

But for the first time in my life I didn't even feel like telling jokes. Mum gave me a big hug when I went up to room 608. She sent Mack out for a special Kentucky chicken tea.

'To make up for last night, lovie,' said Mum. 'Sorry about that. And Mack's sorry he got snappy too. He's feeling better now.'

Mack might be feeling better, Mum might be feeling better. I didn't feel better at all.

I normally love Kentucky chicken take-aways. I like to sit cross-legged on the floor with Pippa and kid on we're American pioneers like in *Little House on the Prairie*, and we're eating a chicken our Pa has raised and there are prowling bears outside who can smell it cooking but we're safe inside our little log cabin.

'Play our game,' Pippa commanded, but somehow I couldn't make it work.

I usually finish off the game by pretending Hank is a baby bear cub and we all feed him bits of chicken (Hank loves this game too) and then we have a jolly sing-song. But now I didn't feel I ever wanted to sing again.

I didn't want to say anything.
I didn't want to tell jokes.
I didn't want to be me.

'Do try and cheer up, Elsa,' said Mum. 'Come on, you're going to have to go to bed if you sulk around the room like this.'

'I don't care,' I said.

So I went to bed really early, before Pippa – even before Hank. Of course it was difficult to get to sleep when the light was on and the telly was loud and there were two and a half people and a baby still racketing round the room, but I put my head way down under the covers and curled up in a little ball with my hands over my ears.

When I woke up I couldn't hear anything even when I took my hands away. I stuck my head out the covers. I could hardly see anything either in the dark. It seemed like the middle of the night.

And yet . . . someone was cooking supper somewhere. I could smell chips. People sometimes stayed up really late and made midnight snacks. I licked my lips. I hadn't eaten all my Kentucky chicken because I'd felt so fed up. I could do with a little snack now myself.

I wondered who was cooking in the kitchen. I'd got to know most of our sixth floor by now. Most of them were quite matey with me. I wondered if they'd consider sharing a chip or two.

I eased myself out of bed. Pippa mumbled

something in her sleep, but didn't wake up. I picked my way across the crowded floor, tripping over Pippa's My Little Pony and stepping straight into a Kentucky chicken carton, but eventually reached the door. I opened it very slowly so that it wouldn't make any noise and crept outside into the corridor. Then I stood still, puzzled. There was a much stronger smell now. And there was a strange flickering light coming from right down the end, in the kitchen. And smoke. You don't get smoke without . . . FIRE!

We Nearly Have Our Chips!

For just one second I stood still, staring. And then I threw back my head and gave a great lion roar.

'FIRE!' I shouted. 'FIRE FIRE FIRE!'

I banged on room 612, I banged on room 611, I banged on room 610, I banged on room 609, charging wildly back down the corridor and bellowing all the while.

'FIRE FIRE FIRE FIRE FIRE FIRE FIRE FIRE FIRE!'

I shouted so long and so loud it felt as if there was a fire in my own head, red and roaring. And then I got to room 608 and I went hurtling inside, screaming and shouting as I snapped on the light.

'FIRE!' I flew to Mum and shook her shoulder hard. Mack propped himself up on one elbow, his eyes bleary. 'Shut that racket!' he mumbled.

'I can't! There's a fire along in the kitchen. Oh, quick, quick, Mum, wake up! Pippa, get up, come on, out of bed.'

Mum sat up, shaking her head, still half-asleep. It was Mack who suddenly shot straight out, grabbing Hank from one bed, Pippa from the other.

'It's OK, Elsa. I'll get them out. You wake the others along the corridor,' he said, busy and brisk.

'Oh good lord, what are we going to do?' Mum said, stumbling out of bed, frantic. 'Quick kids, get dressed as soon as you can – I'll do Hank.'

'No, no, there's no time. We've just got to get out,' said Mack. 'No clothes, no toys, no messing about – OUT!'

'Baby Pillow!' Pippa yelled, struggling, but Mack held her tight.

'I've got him,' I said, snatching Baby Pillow from Pippa's bed.

Then I went charging down the corridor, calling, 'FIRE FIRE FIRE!' all over again.

The smoke was stronger now, and I could hear this awful crackling sound down the corridor. One of the men went running towards the kitchen in his pyjamas, but when he got near he slowed down and then backed away.

'Get everyone out!' he shouted. 'The whole kitchen's ablaze. Keep yelling, little kid. Wake them all up, loud as you can.'

I took a huge breath and roared the dreadful warning over and over again. Some people came running out straight away. Others shouted back, and someone started screaming that we were all going to be burnt alive.

'No-one will be burnt alive if you all just stop panicking,' Mack shouted, charging down the corridor, Pippa under one arm, Hank under the other, Mum stumbling along in her nightie behind them. Mack was only wearing his vest and pants and any other time in the world I'd have rolled around laughing, he looked such a sight.

But we all looked sights. People came blundering out of their bedrooms in nighties and pyjamas and T-shirts and underwear. Some were clutching handbags, some had carrier bags, several had shoved their possessions in blankets and were dragging them along the corridor.

'Leave all your bits and bobs behind. Let's just get out down the stairs. Carry the kids. Come on, get cracking!' Mack yelled. He banged his fist against the fire alarm at the end of the corridor and it started ringing.

'You nip down to the fifth floor and get that alarm going too, Elsa!' Mack yelled. 'And keep calling "Fire!" to get that dozy lot woken up properly. Go on, pal, you're doing great.'

I shot off down the stairs and searched for the fifth-floor fire alarm – but it had already been broken weeks ago by some of the boys and no-one had ever got round to mending it. But I wasn't broken. I was in full working order.

'FIRE!' I roared. 'Get up, get out! Come on, wake up! FIRE FIRE FIRE!'

I ran the length of the corridor and back, banging on every door, screeching until my throat was sore. Then I rushed back down the stairs, pushing past sleepy people stumbling in their nightclothes, desperate to find Mum and Pippa and Hank and Mack, wanting to make sure they were safe.

'Elsa! Elsa, where are you? Come here, baby!'

It was Mum, forcing her way back up the stairs, shouting and screaming.

'Oh Elsa!' she cried, and she swooped on me, clutching me as if she could never let me go. 'I thought you were with us – and then I looked back and you weren't there and I had to come back to get you even though Mack kept telling me you were fine and you were just waking everyone up . . . Oh Elsa, lovie, you're safe!'

'Of course I'm safe, Mum,' I said, hugging her fiercely. 'But I've got to get cracking down on the fourth floor now. No-one else has got such a good voice as me. Listen. FIRE!'

I nearly knocked Mum over with the force of my voice.

'Goodness! Yes, well, I don't see how anyone can sleep through that. But it's OK, they've got the other fire alarms going now and some of the men are seeing that everyone's getting out. They've rung for the fire engines. So come on now, darling – hang on tight to my hand,' said Mum.

We made our way down the stairs, clinging to each other. There was no smoke down on the lower floors but people were still panicking, surging out and running like mad, pushing and shoving. One little kid fell down but his mum pulled him up again and one of the men popped him up on his shoulders out of harm's way. The stairs seemed to go on for ever, as if we were going down and down right into the middle of the earth, but at last the lino changed to the cord carpeting of the first floor and then even though our feet kept trying to run downwards, we were on the level of the ground floor.

The Manager was there in a posh camel dressing gown, wringing his hands.

'Which one of you crazies set my hotel on fire?' he screamed. 'I'll have the law on you!'

'And we'll have the law on you too, because your fire alarms aren't working properly and we could all have got roasted to a cinder if it wasn't for my kid,' Mack thundered. He was still clutching Pippa in one arm, Hank in another. He turned to me – and for one mad moment I thought he was going to try to pick me up too. 'Yeah, this little kid here! She raised the alarm. She got us all up and out of it. Our Elsa.'

I'm not Mack's Elsa and I never will be – but I didn't really mind him showing off about me all the same.

'That Elsa!'

'Yes, little Elsa – she yelled "Fire!" fit to bust.'

'She was the one who woke us up – that little kid with the loud voice.'

They were all talking about me as we surged outside the hotel on to the pavement. Lots of people came and patted me on the back and said I'd done a grand job, and one man saw I was shivering out in the cold street and wrapped his jumper right round me to keep me warm. Someone had dragged out a whole pile

179

of blankets and the old ladies and little kids got first pick. There weren't enough to go round.

'Come on, Jimmy, you can be a gent too,' said Mack, seizing hold of the Manager and 'helping' him out of his cosy camel dressing gown. He draped it round a shivery Asian granny who nodded and smiled. The Manager was shaking his head and frowning ferociously. He looked even sillier than Mack now, dressed in a pair of silky boxer shorts and nothing else. The bunny receptionist looked a bit bedraggled too without her angora jumper and with her fluffy hair in curlers. Switchboard looked startling in red satin pyjamas – a bit like a large raspberry jelly. Now that everyone was safe out in the street this fire was almost starting to be fun.

Then we heard a distant clanging and a big cheer went up. The fire engines were coming! We all crowded out of their way, and firemen in yellow helmets went rushing into the hotel with all their firefighting equipment. Lots of the kids wanted to go rushing in after them to watch. Funny-Face had to be frogmarched away by his mum, and Simple Simon and Nicky and Neil started their own fire-engine imitations, barging around bumping into people. Even baby Hank cottoned on and started shrieking like a siren.

Several ambulances arrived although no-one had actually been hurt, and the police came too. And guess who else? A television crew. Not the *Children in Crisis* people. These were from one of the news stations. And there were reporters too, running around with notebooks, and photographers flashing away with their cameras although all the people in their underwear started shrieking. Everyone asked how the fire started and who discovered it and someone said 'Elsa' and then someone else echoed them and soon almost everyone was saying 'Elsa Elsa Elsa'.

Me!

People were prodding me, pushing me forwards towards the cameras and the microphones and the notebooks. It was my Moment of Glory.

And do you know what? I can hardly bear to admit it. I came over all shy. I just wanted to duck my head and hide behind my mum.

'Come on now, lovie. Tell us all about it. You were the one who raised the alarm, weren't you? Come on, sweetheart, no need to be shy. It sounds as if you've been very brave,' they said. 'Tell us in your own words exactly what happened.'

I opened my mouth. But no words came out. It was as if I'd used up all my famous voice yelling 'Fire!' so many times.

So someone else started speaking for me. The wrong someone. The someone who really doesn't have anything to do with me. We're not even related. Though now he was acting as if he was my dad and I was his daughter.

'The poor wee girl's still a bit gob-smacked – and no wonder! My, but she did a grand job raising the alarm,' Mack boasted, strutting all around. He was careful to hold in his tummy

all the time the cameras were pointing his way. He couldn't flex his arm muscles properly because he was still carrying Pippa and Hank, but he kept carefully arranging his legs as if he was posing for Mister Universe. He didn't half look a berk. He sounded a right berk too, prattling on and on about his wee Elsa. If I'd had any voice left at all I'd have contradicted him furiously.

Then little Pippa piped up.

'Yes, my sister Elsa's ever so big and brave. She rescued my baby!'

'She rescued the baby?' said the reporters, looking at Hank.

'Yep, she went and got him out of his cot. I was crying and crying because I thought he'd get all burnt up and Dad and Mum wouldn't let me go back for him—'

'They wouldn't go back for the *baby*?' said the reporters, their eyes swivelling from Hank to Mum and Mack.

'Not *our* baby. It's just Pippa's pillow. She calls it her baby,' said Mum quickly. Then she realized the cameras were aiming at her, and she clutched her nightie with one hand and did her best to tidy her hair with the other. 'Don't worry, we made sure we had our baby Hank safe and sound. But certainly if it hadn't been for our Elsa then we could still be in our beds right this minute – charred to cinders,' said Mum dramatically.

'Yes, Elsa banged on our door and woke us all up. We'd be dead if it wasn't for her. She rescued all of us,' said Naomi's mum.

'Me and all *my* babies,' she said, showing them off to the camera.

'Elsa's my best friend,' said Naomi, nodding her head so that her plaits jiggled.

'Elsa's *my* best friend too and she rescued us and all,' said Funny-Face, and then he pulled the funniest face he could manage, all cross-eyes and drooly mouth until his mum gave him a poke.

My mum was giving me a poke too.

'Come on then, pet. Haven't you got anything to say for yourself? All these nice gentlemen want you to say a few words about the fire. Come on, lovie, this is your big chance,' Mum hissed.

I knew it. I swallowed. I wet my lips. I took a deep breath.

'Fire,' I mumbled. It was as if my voice could still only say one thing. I concentrated fiercely, trying to gain control. Fire crackled through my thoughts. My brain suddenly glowed.

'Do you know what happened to the plastic surgeon who got too close to the fire?' I said, in almost my own voice.

185

'What plastic surgeon? There was a medical man in there? Did he get out OK?' the reporters clamoured.

'He melted!' I said, and fell about laughing.

They blinked at me, missing a beat.

I decided to forge right ahead like a true professional.

'What were the two Spanish firemen called?'

'We haven't got any Spaniards in our team,' said one of the firemen, wiping the sweat from his brow and replacing his helmet.

'OK, but what would they be called? Hosé and Hose B! Do you get it?'

He didn't look very sure. Mum gave me a violent nudge.

'Elsa, stop telling those silly *jokes*!'

But once I got started I couldn't ever seem to stop.

'Why did the fireman wear red trousers?' I paused for a fraction. Everyone was still staring at me oddly. 'His blue ones were at the cleaners!'

'Pack it in, Elsa,' Mack hissed, looking like he wasn't so sure he wanted me to be his wee Elsa after all.

'It's the shock,' said Mum firmly. 'She's just having a funny five minutes.'

'Only she's not being flipping funny,' said Mack.

186

'Yep, I think we'd better cut the jokes,' said the television man gently.

'I'll try harder,' I said desperately. 'I'll try a new set of jokes, OK? Or I could put on a silly voice . . . ?'

'Why not use your own voice, Elsa? And why do you have to try so hard? Just be yourself. Act natural,' said the television man, chucking me under the chin. 'Let's start again, hmm? Tell us in your own words exactly what happened.'

'But if I just say any old thing, without any jokes, then I'm not funny,' I wailed.

'Who says you've got to be funny?'

'Well, I want to be a comedienne and get to be famous.'

'You don't have to be funny to be famous. And we don't really want people chortling when this goes out on the news. We want to touch the heart. We've got a super story here. You're a great little kid, Elsa. You'll come over really well on television if you just *relax*.'

'It's kind of difficult to act relaxed when you're standing on the pavement in your T-shirt and knickers and a whole bunch of strangers are asking you questions,' I said, sighing.

I wasn't trying to be funny. But the weirdest thing happened. Everyone chuckled appreciatively.

'So what happened, Elsa? You woke up in the middle of the night and . . . ?'

And so I started to tell them exactly what happened. I said I thought the smell was someone cooking chips and I started to get peckish and slipped out of bed to go and beg a few chips for myself. (They laughed again.) Then I told about tripping over Pippa's My Little Pony. (More laughter – and I still hadn't told a single joke!) Then I went on about the fire and dashing up and down the corridor banging on the doors and yelling. (I waited for them to laugh again, but this time they listened spellbound.) The television man asked what I'd yelled and I said 'Fire' and he said that wasn't very loud and *I* said well, I did it a lot louder. And he said show us. So I did. I threw back my head and roared.

'F-I-I-I-I-I-I-I-I-I-I-I-I-I-I-I-I-I-I-I-R-E!!!'

That nearly blew them all backwards. Most people had their hands over their ears. Some shook their heads, dazed. Then someone laughed. They all joined in. Someone else cheered. Someone else did too. Lots of cheers. For me. FOR ME!

It really was my Moment of Fame. I hadn't blown it after all.

My interview went out on the television. I thought I sounded sort of stupid, but everyone else said it went splendidly. (Well, Mum moaned because her hair was a sight and she didn't have any make-up on, and Mack fussed because they'd cut out most of his bits and he was only shown from the waist up so no-one could see his great hairy legs.) But they didn't cut *any* of my bits.

I might not have made it into the *Children in Crisis* documentary. But guess what. My news interview was repeated later in the year in a special compilation programme called *Children of Courage*. And I got to do another interview with a nice blonde lady with big teeth, and Mum spent some of Mack's betting money on a beautiful new outfit from the Flowerfields Shopping Centre for my special telly appearance. Mum made me try on lots of frilly frocks but they all looked *awful*.

So she gave up and let me choose instead. I wanted black jeans (so they wouldn't show the dirt). Mum bought me a black top too, and tied her red scarf round my neck, and then guess what we found at a car-boot sale? Red cowboy boots! They were a bit big but we stuffed the toes with paper and I looked absolutely great.

The blonde lady with the big teeth loved my outfit too. She said I looked just like a cowboy. I was a bit nervous so without thinking I got launched into a cowboy joke routine.

'Who wears a cowboy hat and spurs and lives under the sea? Billy the Squid!'

She laughed! It wasn't *that* funny, one of my oldest jokes actually, but she laughed and laughed and laughed. She said she loved jokes, the older and cornier the better, and she said I could maybe come on her special show one day and do my own comedy routine !!!!!

We couldn't go back to bed in room 608 when the firemen put the fire out at last. It wasn't all burnt to bits. It was only the kitchen that had cooked itself into little black crumbs. But the whole corridor was thick with smoke and sloshy with water and all the rooms looked as if someone had run amok with giant paint-brushes and vats of black paint. All our stuff was covered in this black treacle, and there was a sharp smell that scratched at your nostrils.

'Sorry, folks. You'll have to stay in temporary accommodation for a few weeks,' said the Chief Fireman, shaking his head.

He looked surprised when all the residents of the Royal gave a hearty cheer. The Manager was prancing about in his silk boxer shorts, pointing out that only a few of the rooms were seriously fire damaged, and that the first few floors were barely affected. There was a lot of rushing around consulting, and eventually it

191

was decided that only the people living on the top two floors need be evacuated.

Us sixth-floor and fifth-floor people hugged and danced and shouted. All the other residents booed and argued and complained. Naomi and I had a big hug because she's on the fifth floor so she could come too. Then Funny-Face came and clapped hands with me because though he's on the fourth floor their room is right below the burnt kitchen and water had swirled right down through the room underneath and was dripping through to them, so they couldn't stay either.

We were all ferried off in police cars and coaches to this church hall, where several big bossy ladies with cardigans over their nighties handed out blankets and pillows and sleeping bags. They gave us paper cups of hot soup too – which we needed, because the church hall was freezing. The floor was slippery lino and fun to skid across in your socks, but not exactly cosy or comfy when we settled down to go to sleep. I didn't exactly rate bed number eight – and it soon got crowded because Pippa unzipped my sleeping bag and stuck herself in too. She kept having nightmares and twitching and I had to keep waking her up and dragging her off to the toilet because I was all too aware of what would happen if I didn't.

There was only one toilet and there were queues for it all night long. It was worse in the morning. There was only the one small wash-basin too, and most people didn't have their toothbrushes or flannels or towels anyway.

'I don't know why we were flipping cheering last night,' said Mum, trying to wipe round Hank's sticky face with a damp hankie. 'Compared with this draughty old dump the Royal is practically a palace.'

'We can't stay here,' said Mack, sitting up and scratching. 'I'm going right down that Housing Department first thing.'

'Oh yeah?' said Mum, looking at him. 'You're walking down the road in your underpants, right? Don't forget you haven't even got any trousers any more. And look at me! This is all I've got – the old nightie that I'm wearing. All my clothes, all my make-up, my crinoline-lady ornament . . . all gone! Even if they're not ruined by that smoke then someone will be bound to nick them before I can get back to claim them.' She started to cry so I went and put my arms round her.

'Don't cry, Mum,' I said, hugging her tight.

'You've still got us.'

Mum snuffled a bit but then hugged me back.

'Yes, that's right, Elsa. I've still got my family. My Mack. My baby. My little girl. And my special big girl.'

The special big girl went a bit snuffly herself then. I was glad that Funny-Face in the next row of sleeping bags was still fast asleep or he might have jeered. He looked oddly little, snuggled up under the blanket. And he sucked his thumb and all!

More big bossy ladies breezed into the hall and started heating up a big urn of tea. They had lots of packets of biscuits too. I helped hand them round to everyone. We could have seconds and even thirds. A Bourbon, a shortbread finger and a chocolate Hob Nob make quite a good breakfast.

Then the ladies started dragging in great black plastic sacks crammed with clothes.

'Come and help yourselves! There should be enough for a new outfit for everyone.'

'Oh, big deal,' Mum grumbled. 'It's just tatty old junk left over from jumbles. I'm not wearing anyone's old Crimplene cast-offs.'

She watched Funny-Face's mum trying to squeeze herself into a tight black skirt.

'She's wasting her time. She'll never get that

over her big bum,' Mum mumbled, and when Funny-Face's mum had to give up the attempt, Mum darted out and snatched the skirt herself.

'There! I thought so! That's a Betty Barclay skirt. I've seen them on sale in Flowerfields. Hey, look, does it fit?' Mum pulled it up over her narrow hips and stood preening. 'I wonder if there's a jacket to go with it, eh?'

Mum started skimming her way through the plastic sacks and came up with all sorts of goodies – even a pair of patent high heels her exact size. She had more trouble finding stuff for Mack, considering the only size he takes is *out*-size. She found a jumper that could just about go round him, but the biggest trousers could barely do up and the legs ended way above his ankles. Hank was a bit of a problem too – there were heaps of baby clothes, but he's such a *big* baby that the average one-year-old's sleeping suit came unpopped every time he breathed out and bent him up double into the bargain. Pippa was fine, fitting all the little frocks a treat, but I looked such a fool in the only one my size that Mum threw it back in the pile. (Naomi tried it on instead and looked gorgeous, but then she always does.) Funny-Face was delving in a sack of boys' clothes so I had a sift through too and found some jeans

and a jumper and a really great baseball
bomber jacket with a picture of a lion on the
back!

'Well, we're all kitted out like a dog's dinner,
but we've still got no place to go,' said Mack.

But he was wrong.

Oh, you'll never guess where we ended up!

Someone from the Social and the man from
the Housing Office came round to the church
hall to tell us. We were all going to be temporarily accommodated in another hotel. Not a
special bed-and-breakfast DHS dumping
ground. A *real* hotel. The Star Hotel. With
stars after its name.

When we stepped through those starry glass doors it was like finding fairyland. There were soft sofas all over the reception area, and thick red carpet and flowers in great vases, and a huge chandelier sparkled from the ceiling. All us lot from the Oyal Htl crowded into the reception area, and Mum and Mack and Naomi's mum and Funny-Face's mum and dad and all the other grown-ups sprawled on the sofas while we all ran round and round the red carpet and up and down the wide staircase and rang all the bells on the lifts.

The Star Manager came out of his office to meet us. He didn't look terribly thrilled to see us, but he shook us all by the hand, even the littlest stickiest kid, and welcomed us to the Star Hotel. Then there was a lot of hoo-ha and argy-bargy about rooms, with the Manager and his chief receptionist going into a huddle. This receptionist was dark instead of blonde, and fierce instead of fluffy, but she also had long pointy fingernails and she started to tap them very impatiently indeed. But at last it was all sorted out and she handed all of us little cards instead of keys.

We were in suite 13. It might be an unlucky number for some people, but it was lucky lucky lucky for us.

Note I said suite, not room. As we shot up one floor in the lift and padded along the thickly carpeted corridor, Pippa licked her lips hopefully, thinking we were going to be given a sweety sweet. Even I didn't twig what suite really meant.

Suite 13 wasn't just one room. It was a set of

three rooms, just like a little flat. Only there was nothing little about suite 13. It was really big – and *beautiful*. The main room was blue, with deeper blue velvet curtains and a dark blue coverlet on the huge bed. There was a painting on the wall of a boy in a blue velvet suit and a blue glass vase on the bedside table filled with little blue pretendy rosebuds. There was a dressing table with swivel mirrors so you could see the back of your head, and a blue leather folder containing notepaper and envelopes, and a blue felt-tip pen patterned with stars. There was a big television too – a colour one – and it even had Sky!

There was a bathroom leading off this main room. It was blue too, with a blue bath, blue basin, even a blue loo. They all shone like the sea they were so sparkly clean. Laid out on the gleaming tiled shelf were little blue bottles of shampoo and bath gel and tiny cakes of forget-me-not soap. Mum sniffed them rapturously, her eyes shining.

Mack kicked his shoes off and lay on the big bed, Hank sitting astride his tummy. The bed was so big that even Mack could fit right inside it, and his feet wouldn't stick out at the end. I thought we might *all* have to fit inside it, because it was the only bed in the room.

Then I saw another door and opened it. There was another bedroom, with three single beds, three little beside tables, and three little wooden chairs with carved hearts and painted roses. It was just like the three bears fairy story – and there were bears on the duvets too, and a painting of Goldilocks up on the wall. The carpet and wallpaper were pale blue but the ceiling was a deep navy, with stars scattered all over it. That night when I slept in my wonderful, soft, splendid bed number nine I could still see the stars, even with the light switched off. They glowed luminously in the dark, my own magic midnight stars. I didn't want to sleep, just in case this was all a wonderful dream and when I woke up I'd be back in the grotty old Oyal Htl.

But it wasn't a dream at all. I woke up early and lay luxuriating in my bed and then I crept into Mum and Mack's room. They were all cuddled up together, looking friendly even though they were fast asleep. I sat down at the dressing table and practised a few funny faces and then I took a piece of paper and the felt-tip pen and wrote letters to all my friends.

*** Star Hotel ***

Dear Jamie,
    I hope you haven't forgot me, I'm Elsa, and I don't like my new school much but I do like my new home. It's ever such a posh hotel and if it's nearer your school maybe I can come back which would be GREAT.

                Love from Elsa
P.S. I'm the girl they said was thick but you said I was INTELLIGENT.

★★★ Star Hotel ★★★

Dear Mrs Hoover, Sorry
Mrs Macpherson,
    Hey, this hotel is
HEAPS better than the Royal.
Why don't you come and work
here? I bet you'd like it and
I'd give you a hand. The walls
have all got fancy paper so
no-one ever scribbles on them.
            Love from Elsa

★★★ Star Hotel ★★★

Dear Naomi,
    Isn't it super here. My
bedroom's got stars on the
ceiling, has yours? I hope we
don't have to go back to the
Royal for ages and ages.
See you at breakfast.
        Love from your friend Elsa
                X X X

★★★ Star Hotel ★★★

Dear Funny-Face,
    There are lots of bushes
and trees and stuff at the
end of the Star Hotel garden
so maybe we could make
a camp ???
            See you.
                Elsa

★★★ Star Hotel ★★★

Dear Pippa,
    I will read you this let
seeing as you can't read
yet yourself. It is from me
Elsa, and it's just to say
HELLO and we'll play lots
today.
        Love from your big siste
                Elsa

× × × × × × × × × × × × ×

★★★ Star Hotel ★★★

Dear Hank,
   Hello Big Baby

Love from your big
sister Elsa

   X X X

★★★ Star Hotel ★★★

Dear Mum,
   It's so lovely here I don't
think you'll ever be sad
or cross ever again, eh ?
   Lots and lots of love
      from Elsa

   ×××××××××××××

★★★ Star Hotel ★★★

Dear Mack,
   Och Aye the Noo.
That's all the Scotch
   I know.
         From Elsa

★★★ Star Hotel ★★★

Dear Elsa,
   I am having a lovely time
here. I have been writing
lots and lots of letters. I even
wrote one to the warthog !!!
   But I am too happy to hate
anyone and there are stars
on my ceiling and I have
stars in my eyes because it
is so super here at the Star
Hotel.   Love and ×××
      from Elsa

There! I used up all the notepaper and gave myself a big appetite for breakfast.

Ooooh the breakfast! You have it in a lovely room with a dark pink swirly carpet and pink fuzzy paper on the walls and rose-pink cloths on the tables. You sit at a table and spread a rose-pink napkin on your lap and a waitress in a black frock and a white apron comes and asks what you want to drink. Then you go and help yourself to whatever you want to eat from the breakfast bar. You can have whatever you want. Lots and lots and lots of it.

Even Mum had more breakfast than usual. She had freshly squeezed orange juice and black coffee and toast and butter and marmalade.

Mack had tea and a bowl of porridge because he's Scottish and then he had a big plate of

bacon and egg and mushroom and fried potatoes and more bacon because that's his
favourite, and he tucked the extra bacon into
toast to make a bacon butty.

Pippa didn't copy me! She chose all by herself. Apple juice and Cocoa Pops and milk and
a soft white roll and butter and honey.

Hank had hot milk and a little bowl of
porridge like his dad and a runny egg and tiny
toast soldiers. He loved this breakfast and
wanted to wave his arms about to show his
appreciation and he dropped a few crumbs
(more than a few, actually) on the carpet, but
no-one seemed to mind and the waitress tickled him under the chin and said he was a
chubby little cherub!

Mum and Mack and Pippa and Hank all
knew exactly what they wanted for breakfast.
I was the one who simply couldn't decide
because it all looked so delicious. So guess

what. I had almost all of it.

I had milky tea and cranberry juice and cornflakes sprinkled with rainbow sugar and then muesli with extra sultanas and apple

rings and then scrambled egg on toast with tomato sauce and then sausages stuck in a long roll to make a hot dog and then a big jammy Danish pastry and I ate it all up, every little bit. It was the best breakfast ever.

What with the cranberry juice and the cherry jam in the pastry I ended up looking like Dracula. And that reminded me of a Dracula breakfast joke and that got me started.

I told jokes to Mum and Mack and Pippa and Hank and I shouted them to Naomi and Funny-Face across the tables and I tried them out on our waitress too because she seemed

friendly and she said I was a proper caution.
Do you want to hear a small sample?

What does Dracula like for breakfast?
Readyneck.

What do ghosts like for breakfast?
Dreaded wheat.

What do cannibals like for breakfast?
Buttered host.

What do Frenchmen eat for breakfast?
Huit heures bix.

How would a cannibal describe a man in a
hammock?
Breakfast in bed.

What happens when a baby eats Rice Krispies?
It goes snap, crackle and poop.

I *must* stop rabbiting on like this. Well.
Just one more.

What do you get if you pour boiling water
down a rabbit hole?

Hot cross bunnies!

I'm not hot. I feel super-cool.
I'm not cross. I'm happy happy happy.
I'm not a bunny. I'm Elsa and I roar like a lion.

Hey, what do you get if you cross a lion with a parrot?
I don't know, but if he says 'Pretty Polly' you'd better

SMILE

☆ THE BED AND ☆ BREAKFAST STAR

I think Elsa is one of the cheeriest, kindest children I've ever invented. She has such a tough time too. Her mum is so tired and depressed she hasn't got much time for her and her stepdad is a bit of a scary nightmare. Elsa is expected to look after her half-siblings Pippa and Hank and generally make herself useful. It's very grim losing your house and having to stay in bed and breakfast accommodation but Elsa adapts rapidly and makes the best of the situation.

Sometimes she's a little too relentlessly cheery. She wants to be a comedian when she grows up so she tries her hardest to be funny all the time, endlessly cracking jokes. She's not very good at making up her own jokes just yet so she tells really awful old corny jokes that make you groan.

I'm not very good at making up jokes either. I knew I'd need lots and lots of silly jokes for Elsa, and wondered what I was going to do. Then one day when I was giving a talk to some children. I told them I was writing a new book about a funny girl who kept cracking jokes, and asked if anyone knew a really good joke. There was suddenly a forest of waving hands. I got out my notebook and started scribbling down all their suggestions. I couldn't write all of them down. The funniest were frequently too rude and naughty to be put in a children's book!

I used to live in a street where there were several bed and breakfast hotels for homeless families. I could see it was very tough for any adults in that situation, but the children seemed to be able to make the most of it and have fun, just like Elsa. I used to bump into them in the sweet shop and the video and DVD shop and have a little chat. They'd often make me crack up laughing.

They were always eating chocolate and crisps and chips, quick easy food. Elsa has a very healthy appetite (though her diet isn't exactly a healthy one!) It was fun choosing all the food she'd like best. Then at the end, when the whole family is staying in the swish Star hotel I loved deciding what they'd all choose for their very elaborate breakfasts.

Elsa ends up a real heroine and gets to be on television, interviewed by a lady who cares passionately about children and has a weakness for silly jokes herself. I based her on the well known television personality, Esther Rantzen. I'd never met her when I wrote the book, but now I'm proud to say that I've been given a Childline award and Esther has become a special friend.

Jacqueline Wilson

☆ HOW WELL DO YOU ☆
KNOW ELSA?

Who is Elsa named after?

What's the name of the hotel where
Elsa lives with her family?

Who is Naomi hiding from when
Elsa meets her in the bathroom?

What is Pippa's favourite toy?

What's the title of the book Naomi
disguises as *Little Women*?

What word does Funny-Face
have to write out fifty times as
a punishment at school?

What does Elsa first mistake
the smell of the fire for?

Which TV show does Elsa end up on?

What's the name of the lovely hotel
where Elsa and her family live
after the fire?

What do ghosts like for breakfast?

Answers:

Elsa the lion; The Royal Hotel; her brothers; Baby Pillow
– a pillow!; *The Cursed Werewolf*; CLASSROOM; chips;
Children of Courage; The Star Hotel; dreaded wheat!

There are six differences between these two
pictures of Elsa – can you spot them all?

☆ ELSA'S FUNNY FACTS! ☆

The Guinness World Record for the most jokes told in one minute is held by Clive Greenaway, who managed a total of 26! Clive had to practice for months to get his routine perfect – and every one of the jokes had to get laughter from the audience to be counted for the record.

Have you ever laughed so much you couldn't stop? There's a famous recording of Elvis Presley singing the song 'Are You Lonesome Tonight?' in front of a live audience on 26 August 1969 and breaking down with uncontrollable laughter – apparently he was amused either by the sight of an audience member taking off his toupee, or by the warbling of one of his backing singers!

Babies first smile at the age of six weeks, and they first start to giggle at about the age of three and a half months, though it can take up to the age of nine months before a baby starts to laugh.

☆ ELSA'S STAR BREAKFAST ☆ WORD SEARCH

There are ten delicious breakfast items hidden
in the grid below – can you find them all?

F	D	J	U	R	A	G	U	S	P	F	U	W	S	I
H	G	Q	T	X	U	H	K	N	K	Z	T	M	E	T
U	S	T	S	S	F	M	B	G	Z	H	P	S	K	L
P	E	Y	A	P	G	X	L	T	C	O	E	B	A	T
C	U	Z	K	B	A	G	A	O	F	G	L	Y	L	V
O	Z	Z	H	A	N	S	E	U	A	W	H	J	F	O
M	U	E	S	L	I	F	T	S	F	O	F	U	N	E
S	J	H	S	D	C	H	U	R	A	N	P	I	R	H
E	L	N	P	H	N	A	Y	B	Y	P	T	C	O	A
A	F	F	U	O	S	F	P	P	A	P	W	E	C	Y
D	H	B	T	T	Q	L	O	T	H	O	N	E	M	W
E	U	I	S	X	E	X	D	C	P	O	B	R	A	B
Q	Y	P	O	R	K	O	B	M	N	G	A	P	G	G
R	U	L	S	L	J	C	A	U	O	I	P	E	T	Z
S	X	U	M	H	I	J	I	M	Q	P	W	C	H	D

APPLE   CORNFLAKES   EGG   JAM   JUICE
MUESLI   TEA   PASTRY   SAUSAGES   SUGAR

☆ VISIT THE WEBSITE ☆

There's a whole Jacqueline Wilson town to explore!
You can generate your own special username,
customize your online bedroom, test
your knowledge of Jacqueline's books
with fun quizzes and puzzles, and
upload book reviews. There's lots
of fun stuff to discover, including
competitions, book trailers, and
Jacqueline's scrapbook. And if
you love writing, visit the special
storytelling area!

Plus, you can hear the latest news
from Jacqueline in her monthly
diary, find out whether she's doing
events near you, read her fan-mail
replies, and chat to other fans on
the message boards!

www.jacquelinewilson.co.uk

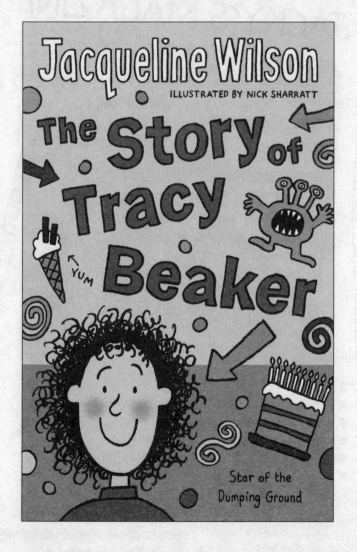

Jacqueline Wilson

ILLUSTRATED BY NICK SHARRATT

The Story of Tracy Beaker

YUM

Star of the
Dumping Ground